ARMAGH
FOLK
TALES

T0352785

ARMAGH
FOLK
TALES

FRANCES QUINN

The
History
Press
Ireland

For
my father
Mick the Tailor

and

my brother
Pat
alias John Patrick

both moulded out of
Armagh clay

First published 2014, reprinted 2015

The History Press Ireland
50 City Quay
Dublin 2
Ireland
www.thehistorypress.ie

British Library Cataloguing in Publication Data.
A catalogue record for this book is available from the British Library.

ISBN 978 1 84588 814 5

Typesetting and origination by The History Press
Printed and bound by TJ Books Ltd, Padstow, Cornwall

CONTENTS

ACKNOWLEDGEMENTS

I'd like to thank all of the following for their encouragement and/
or their generosity in providing or sharing material and memories:

Davey Armstrong; Seán Barden; Jim Blaney; Ruairí and Brenda
Blaney; Seán Boylan (Keady); Colette and Mark; Martin
Conlon; Paddy Corrigan; Molly Cunningham; Charlie Dillon
(Snr); Eileen Fagan; Seán and Maura Farrell; Pat Fairon; Mary
Flanagan; Ann Gilmartin; Rosemary Gohan; Dermot Hicks;
Eileen Hicks; Mary Hughes; Patricia Kennedy; Madeleine and
Peter Kelly; Denis Lavery; Josephine and Peter Mackle; Seán
McAteer; Criostóir Mac Carthaigh; Vincent McKeever; Pat
Joe McKenna; Pat McNally; Mary McVeigh; Phil Mohan; Kay
Muhr; Kevin Murphy; Mgr Raymond Murray; Colette O'Brien;
Fergal and Joan O'Brien; Finn O'Gorman; Bernard O'Hanlon;
John Pearson; Arthur Quinn; Margery Quinn; Michael Quinn;
Greer Ramsey; Jim Smart; Jean Trainor; Hilda Winter; the staff
of Armagh County Museum; The Irish Studies Library,
Armagh; The Cardinal Ó Fiaich Memorial Library; the staff of
The Folklore Commission, University College Dublin and Peter
Carson of the Ulster Folk and Transport Museum. Lastly, a very
special thanks to Patricia McConville.

PERMISSIONS

My thanks to:

Peter Murphy and the Murphy family for kind permission to reprint collected items in *Now You're Talking* and *My Man Jack* by Michael J. Murphy.

Dundalgan Press for kind permission to reprint collected items from T.G.F. Paterson's *Country Cracks*.

Patricia Kennedy for kind permission to retell her stories from her *Of Other Days Around Us*.

ILLUSTRATIONS

All illustrations are by the author.

INTRODUCTION

Some places have gold or silver mines. In Armagh our real riches lie in song and story. Seam after seam of them we have and this book is but a narrow shaft into the cultural riches of the county.

Like many counties in Ireland, stories are in the DNA of the people. The landscape is the fabric of the stories – what sews us together or unfortunately, at times, rips us apart. Stories are a way of coming to terms with our fortunes and misfortunes, and with the quirks of others; in short, a way of making sense of the human condition. It comes naturally in Ireland to be creative with language, to order a story to amuse or impress. What I think is so great about our local stories is their obvious delight in the infinite variety of human nature: from solid legends to fey fairy stories and tales which show how we relish eccentricity. Folk stories are such a great antidote to the packaged conformity and image-conscious society of today.

In putting together this collection of stories, I wanted to pay tribute to two folklorists from County Armagh: T.G.F. Paterson and Michael J. Murphy. I don't think these two remarkable men have received anything like the acknowledgement they deserve. Kevin Murphy, in his article 'The Last Druid', said that Patrick Kavanagh's remark, 'I flew to knowledge, without going to college' applied equally to Michael J. Murphy. Interestingly enough it applies to both Murphy and Paterson because both men left school around the age of fourteen and went on to amazing achievements and to write books. Both were offered OBEs, which Paterson accepted and Murphy declined, reflecting two points on a wide spectrum of allegiance and political outlook that exists in the North.

I have included in the collection a number of colloquial accounts taken mostly from Paterson's *Country Cracks* and Murphy's *Now You're Talking*. I see no point in changing rich local language into an anodyne standard one – society already abounds in strangulated vowels and attempts to reject regionality. I have made further mention of some of their stories in the hope that it will whet people's appetite to go back to the very enjoyable writings of both men and I frequently make reference to Paterson's *Harvest Home* – a real treasure trove.

While I was working on this project I spoke to many, many Armagh people and there wasn't one occasion when it didn't add to my knowledge and understanding of the place. Although it wasn't appropriate to use all the material here, everything went into the mix and helped me enormously. Of course I have only managed to touch on a fraction of the lore of nearly 1,000 townlands!

My aim was not to produce a worthy tome or a book of academic excellence but rather a popular collection – something that is more typical of the people of the county. For this I wanted to include stories that ranged from the sublime to the ridiculous.

It was interesting that the consensus of opinion was that fairies and ghosts had gone out when electric light came in – that they had been part of an unlit country landscape when people had no transport and had to walk home at night on dark lonely roads. Now that we have electric light in houses and streets and all our modern conveniences, we are no longer victims of our imagination. Having quite confidently told me that, the same people went on to tell me about experiences they'd had where they had seen and heard supernatural things!

Before this I'd always heard that it was parents or grandparents or friends of friends who had seen ghosts or knew someone who had seen a fairy. This time – in 2013! – I was talking to people who were telling me about personal first-hand experiences. I did begin to wonder though, what with the fairy folk, the resurrections and the normal ghosts, if there was much room for ordinary folk left in the county.

It does make you reflect on 'the digital age' where the image-conscious are so aware of keeping up with whatever everyone else is keeping up with, that it's necessary for them to spend nearly every minute checking it out by text or online. The reality of the moment and being in the present is forfeited for virtual reality, so we may well be on the way to losing our sensitivity to the atmosphere around us.

Listening to people's experiences of life in the past was an enormously enjoyable experience, especially when it was from seventy-, eighty- and ninety-year-olds and the ninety-year-olds, in particular were so young at heart!

IN CONCILIO · CONSILIUM

1

LEGENDS

THE CHILDREN OF LIR

This story is the best known of the 'three sorrows of storytelling' in Ireland but many people don't know of its connection to County Armagh. Tradition has it that King Lir's dwelling, Sí Finachaidh, lay outside Newtownhamilton.

Long ago, at a time when there were five provinces in Ireland, their representatives gathered to elect a king from their midst. The contenders were: Bodb Dearg, Angus, Ilbrec, Lir and Midir. Bodb Dearg was elected and Lir stormed off in high dudgeon at not having been chosen. The chieftains thought to pursue him and punish him severely for his lack of courtesy and sportsmanship but Bodb Dearg thought better of it and preferred to bide his time for an opportunity to win Lir over.

Some time later Lir's wife fell suddenly ill and after a short period she died. When Lir had spent time grieving for her, Bodb Dearg thought that he might take this opportunity to befriend him in his time of need. He invited him to visit and to take one of his foster daughters as a wife to console him in his grief. These young women were the three daughters of Aillil of the islands in Galway Bay. When Lir arrived from Sí Finachaidh with a large band of followers he was welcomed by Bodb Dearg and introduced to three beautiful young women in Bodb Dearg's palace. Spoilt for choice, he could only think to choose Eve, the eldest, saying that she must be the noblest. He spent some time in the court of Bodb Dearg getting to know them all, but especially Eve, and then he brought her back with him to Sí Finachaidh to celebrate their union with a royal feast.

Some time later she gave birth to twins, a boy and a girl, whom they called Fionnuala and Aed. The children brought great delight to them and to the whole court and when Eve was due to give birth to twins again, a few years later, the event was eagerly awaited. Although the twin boys, Fiachra and Conn, arrived safely, Eve, tragically, died. Lir was heartbroken and inconsolable now that he had lost two lovely wives.

Only the children could break through the cloud of his grief and they say that, were it not for them, he would have died of sorrow. Bodb Dearg, who had since established a close relationship with Lir through his foster daughter and grandchildren, really felt for him and wondered how he could help. Like everyone else, he adored the children of Lir and he availed of every opportunity to see them. After discreetly giving him time to mourn this second loss he spoke to him, gently suggesting he take Aoife for a companion, stressing that it was not good to bear his sorrow alone.

Aoife was the next of Bodb's foster daughters and who better to look after Lir's children than the sister of his wife? The sad King Lir saw the sense of this and took Aoife for his wife. And indeed she was no disappointment; she looked after both him and the children and showed them great love. In turn Lir's grief faded and he was able to enjoy life again. His children were such a source of delight to him! He had them sleep near him and he rose early in the morning to play with them. It was not only their father who loved them, the whole court did too, as did their grandfather Bodb Dearg and his court, and all who visited were utterly charmed by them.

Although she loved the children of her dead sister dearly, Aoife began to feel neglected by the two men in her life: her husband and foster father. It was with her they should be besotted, she thought, yet their every thought was for the children. Jealousy began to eat at her heart and twist her mind against the children. Jealousy can make one ill and Aoife took to her bed for a year with a mysterious illness. During that time her thoughts festered and her attitude soured towards the children and she carefully planned to behave in the most deceitful and deceptive of ways.

At the end of the year she rose from her bed – apparently cured. She waited until Lir was away from home, then she announced to the children that she was taking them on a surprise visit to their grandfather, Bodb Dearg. The boys were excited but Fionnuala had had a troubling dream the night before, which left her feeling that Aoife did not mean them well.

When they had left Sí Finachaidh far behind Aoife was so maddened and blinded by jealousy and, in turn, hatred, that she drew her servants to one side away from the children. In her mind the children had become the only obstacle standing between her and the love of Lir and Bodb Dearg and she now tried to persuade the servants to kill them.

They were utterly incredulous. Not only would they not do it but they couldn't understand how Aoife could conceive of such a thing. What Aoife went through then can scarcely be imagined: she had voiced her most evil thoughts and had them denounced by her own servants. She was alone in her misery and hatred and so took a sword with the intention of killing herself, but her courage failed her, so in her desperation she decided to use the dark arts which she had gleaned from her foster father.

When they drew alongside Lake Derravaragh (in County Westmeath), she feigned affection for the children and told them they could have a lovely, refreshing swim. The boys, cooped up so long on the journey, rushed excitedly towards the water but Fionnuala, with a sense of dread and foreboding, hung back. Aoife, however, with cruel determination, urged her forward and there was no denying her. As soon as Fionnuala entered the water, Aoife drew a wand from under her cloak and, pointing to one after the other of the children, she cried fearfully:

'Children of Lir, your good fortune is now at an end
From now on your companions will be the birds of the air.
Your home will be a watery one
You will never more tread dry land.'

The children, in alarm, felt their bodies changing. Fionnuala turned back: 'Oh Aoife, for the love you once had for us, don't do this to us!'

'It's done!' cried Aoife.

'Oh Aoife, for the love you have for our father, don't do this to us!' begged Fionnuala.

'It's done!' cried Aoife, knowing that that was why she was doing it.

'Oh Aoife, for the love you had for our mother, don't leave us like this!' pleaded Fionnuala as the arms of the children grew into wings. 'How long must we endure it?'

'You will spend 300 years on Lake Derravaragh, 300 years on the Sea of Moyle and 300 years on the Western ocean, and not until a prince from Connaght marries a princess from Munster and you hear the voice of the bell of a new religion will you regain your human form.'

Then Aoife realised what she had done to her sister's undeserving children and she began to feel remorse.

'The spell is cast,' she said. 'It cannot be undone. I will, however, grant you the gift of beautiful music to calm all minds and you can keep your voices and sensibilities.' Then she fled from the four beautiful white swans. She left her revenge behind her and she went towards her own fate.

When she arrived at Bodb Dearg's he looked around for the children and asked her where they were. What could she do now but lie, although she knew her fate was sealed. She told him Lir had not wanted her to bring them to see their grandfather. Bodb Dearg was concerned; this was not characteristic; there was something wrong. He sent word to Lir in Sí Finachaidh asking him why he hadn't let the children come with Aoife.

The alarm was raised because Lir had been informed that the children had left with Aoife. Everyone was aware of the strange illness she had had and of her recent erratic behaviour. He set off in haste with his followers and was confounded when they passed Lake Derravaragh and heard the voices of his children. They searched all around before realising that the voices came from the four beautiful swans flying above their heads. Fionnuala, always their spokesperson, explained what had happened and Lir urged them to come and live, just as they were, among their own people who would care for them. Fionnuala told him sadly of their sentence to live on water for 900 years. She pressed him and his followers to stay by the lake that night so that they might hear the sweet, otherworldly music of the swans who could chant away their sorrow and bring them peace.

At first light of dawn next morning, Lir stirred and rose and headed south-west to Bodb Dearg's palace and there he confronted Aoife, obliging her to admit her deed of sorcery. He unfolded the evil web of cruelty and deceit before her foster father and instead of the love that Aoife craved from these two men, she met with terrifying vengeance. Bodb Dearg, with his great powers, forced her to declare her worst fear. It was, she said, to be turned into a demon of the air, a horrid thing. Instantly the powerful magician Bodb Dearg sent her spinning and shrieking, hither and thither on every wind to be hurled about in tempests forever more.

From that day on Bodb Dearg and his followers, in the company of Lir and all his people, camped out by Lake Derravaragh to converse with the swans and listen to their healing music. So while the children could not take on their human form, they lived just like humans in the loving company of all their friends and relations. A settlement grew up by the lake and life was tolerable for everyone, in spite of the transformation. But all things must come to an end and one day Fionnuala knew their time was up there. She informed her brothers and all four spoke their last words to Bodb Dearg and Lir. They rose high into the air, hovered, then flew north to the Mull of Kintyre, leaving the lamentation of their people behind.

The grey seas and skies of the Sea of Moyle brought no joy to the children. They were bereft of family and friends and the calm waters of Lake Derravaragh. They had no one to sing their music for and were relentlessly buffeted about in the sudden storms. They spent their time flying between the coasts of Scotland and Ireland. Once, at the sight of a terrible tempest brewing, Fionnuala realised they could well be separated and since being together was the only strength and consolation they had, she arranged that should they get lost in the squall, they were to make their way back to *Carraig na Rón*, the rock of the seals. That would be their meeting place in this hostile environment. They were indeed separated and when the storm quietened, Fionnuala made her way to the rock but found no one there. At daybreak she saw a little speck on the horizon which, to her relief, turned into the shape of her brother Conn, whom she sheltered under her right wing. Soon Fiachra made his weary way towards them and she placed him under her left wing. Apprehensively she scanned the horizon for a sign of her twin brother and her heart rose to meet him when he appeared. She had not lost him after all and they all huddled together on *Carraig na Rón*.

On one occasion they flew up the estuary of the river Bann, searching out an opportunity to get news of their people. They saw a group of horsemen riding along and so they swam in close to where they were and called out to them in their human voices. Once alerted the horsemen stopped in wonder, for they knew these swans must be of their own people. The two sons of Bodb Dearg were among them, Aed the Keenwitted and Fergus the Chess-player, and they knew the whole story of what had happened. The horsemen were delighted to meet them and gave them news that, at that very time, both Bodb Dearg and Lir were feasting at Sí Finachaidh and were very well except for their separation from the children. This was bitter-sweet news to the swans and Fionnuala could not help but raise a lament – keening the difference of their lifestyles. Time ran on and on until the day came when they had served their term in the Sea of Moyle and their last trial of the Western Ocean was due to begin.

On their way to the west, they thought they would fly over their home place, Sí Finachaidh, once again. They longed to see Lir and Bodb Dearg and to see their childhood haunts, so they made for the estate of their father that lies between Keady and Newtownhamilton. To their consternation they saw the crumbling ruin of their former home. It was now an overgrown desolate place and as they rested on Tullynawood Lake they must have thought themselves the most unfortunate creatures in the world, but destiny drove them on to the Western Ocean.

The winds billowed up the waves off the west coast of Ireland so that they came crashing to the shore like angry animals foaming at the mouth and flocks of birds floated and glided on the currents of the wind as it roared and whistled back and forth. Yet the swans found many inlets to shelter in where life was not as harsh as on the open ocean. They found a lake on an island, Inis Glora, off the coast of County Mayo, and they were able to settle there. It wasn't as sheltered as the inland Lake Derravaragh where they had spent what now seemed like 'happy' years, but it was nevertheless infinitely preferable to the wild Atlantic. The lake became known as the Lake of the Birds because if there was no one to enjoy the beautiful, enchanted music of the swans at least all the other birds appreciated it and flocked to the lake to listen.

Time drifted on in this great bird sanctuary until there came a day when the peace was disturbed by a strange, alien sound on this island. The monks, who wrote down the story, speak of the bell that rang out and say it was that of Kemoc, a hermit monk, who had come to live on the island. They say that the birds chanted their music and Kemoc traced the sound to the lake and spoke to them and befriended them. He took them ashore under his protection and linked them together with a silver chain. And so the first part of the spell was broken: they were on dry land.

It happened that Lairgen, a prince of Connacht, wedded a Munster princess and when she came to Connacht and heard the story of the famous swans, she wished them to be brought to her that she might see and hear them for herself. Her husband demurred, knowing that the swans were sacred, but the head-strong woman must have interpreted this as lack of love for her, because she insisted and even threatened to leave him if he didn't grant her request.

Lairgen complied and sent a message to Kemoc, who refused to part with the swans, so the angry prince came in person and stormed into the small church where Kemoc was protecting them. Lairgen pulled them out roughly and broke the silver chain. He watched, horrified, as the beautiful white creatures shed their feathers and wings and long, graceful necks to reveal the shrivelled skin and limbs of four ancient human beings. Lairgen, though but the catalyst, fled in dismay. The monk, Kemoc, offered them the peace and consolation of his new religion, which it's said they accepted.

These old people knew that their time in the world was near completion so Fionnuala asked Kemoc to bury them right there on Inis Glora, where they finished off their long term of suffering. She asked that he place their bodies just as they had sheltered together on *Carraig na Rón*, strengthening one another with their love: Conn on her right, Fiachra on her left and Aed before her (they buried people vertically in those days). And when they died the monk fulfilled her wishes. He wrote their names in Ogham on a stone and placed it over their tomb.

This story has been told for hundreds of years and thousands of Irish people know the story of the Children of Lir.

The Twins of Macha

The name 'Armagh' (Ard Mhacha in Gaelic) owes its origins to a nearby site known as Emain Macha, meaning height of Macha. Emain Macha is known locally as 'The Navan Fort', just 'The Navan' or even 'Emain'. In the second century AD the Greco-Roman Ptolemy appears to have shown its location on his map of Ireland. It also appears in 1602 in maps by the cartographer Richard Bartlett. It is an area of approximately 18 acres enclosed by a bank and ditch. Excavations, started in the 1960s, revealed evidence of Neolithic, late

Bronze Age and Iron Age activity on the site. As well as artefacts from the Bronze Age, four large, decorated, bronze trumpets and several brooches from the Iron Age were found nearby and are now in the National Museum in Dublin. It was thought to be the site of a royal dwelling during the Iron Age and it is the central location for the great epic The Táin Bo Cuailgne *(The Cattle-Raid of Cooley).*

The Táin, as it is familiarly known, has been called 'the Irish Iliad' and has been an inspiration to many writers, not only Synge, Yeats and his mentor Lady Gregory, but to modern-day writers as well. The events in The Táin *take place at a time when King Conor Mac Nessa ruled Ulster from Emain Macha. Traditionally this was thought to have been in the Iron Age but others have suggested that it was 300-400 years later. In any case, it is central to many of the stories I'm about to relate. I haven't included all of the stories here because they involve other counties as well.*

After Christianity came to Ireland, many of these stories were written down in medieval Irish by the monks and one school of thought says that they were based on an oral tradition stretching back hundreds of years before that. Both the early and later stories have been translated by various scholars and have been dated variously to between the 600s and 1200s AD.

Macha is thought to have been alternatively a queen and a woman from the other world. This is the story of the woman from the other world.

Cruinniuc, son of Agnovan of the Ulaidh (the warriors of Ulster), was a wealthy man who owned a great deal of land. He lived in the wilds of the countryside and had four sons. His wife had died and he was very lonely. One day a woman appeared before him and he thought her very beautiful – no doubt her presence in this all-male household was welcome. She started doing chores in the house and in the evening she put everything in order and, finally, she joined Cruinniuc in bed. This pattern went on for months, making Cruinniuc a happy man once again and eventually she became pregnant.

There was a fair held nearby each year: men, women and children went and Cruinniuc decided to go too. While putting on his best clothes and eagerly anticipating the fair, his wife came to him with a warning. She cautioned him not to mention her existence to anyone. He brushed off her warning with laughter, promising he wouldn't, and he set off in great form. The fair was very enjoyable but the excitement reached its peak with the great chariot race at the end. The king's horses were to take part in the competition and when the king's horses won, everyone cheered and shouted and someone roared out, 'Nothing can run as fast as the king's horses!'

'My wife can run as fast as the king's horses!' yelled Cruinniuc, caught up in the moment and forgetting the promise he had made.

Before he knew what was happening he was dragged before the king and his wife was sent for. She received the messenger with alarm because she was due to go into labour. When she went before the king he ordered her to run against his chariot. Silence fell on the great gathering and the blood drained from her face. She turned round and cried out to them in appeal, 'A woman bore every one of you. Wait until I've given birth.'

But the king had no sympathy for her and if anyone else had, they were afraid to speak. She raced against the chariot then and reached the end of the field before the king's horses did. No sooner had she arrived than she sank to the ground and gave birth to twins. That is why the place is known to this day as *Emain Macha* – the Twins of Macha – and at the birth she screamed out that any man who heard her would suffer the pains of childbirth in his own time of need. All the men there and their progeny suffered this affliction for nine generations afterwards.

MACHA MONGRÚAD

A completely different legend is told about Macha – so different that we must assume it is a different Macha, and why not? It would be a sorry state of affairs if future generations decided that there had only been one 'Mary' or 'Jane' living in our era!

This Macha was the daughter of Rúad and was known as Macha Mongrúad. Her father, Rúad, shared the kingship of Ireland with Cimbáeth and Díthorbae. They each took it in turn to rule for seven years. When Díthorbae died, the right of kingship was passed on to his sons. However, when Rúad died, his only child and daughter, Macha, who was herself a considerable warrior, did not receive the same treatment.

Cimbáeth point-blankly refused to let her rule and the two went into battle. Macha defeated him and gained sovereignty. Moreover, when the term of kingship was up, she treated him as he had treated her and would not concede her position, so they engaged in battle once more and yet again she defeated him. Cimbáeth obviously realised his strategy wasn't working so he decided to form a marriage alliance with her. Indeed, in a warrior society, he may have had a sneaking regard for his superior opponent.

This presumably left the sons of Díthorbae out on a limb and they sought outlaws for their companions and together with these they caused great anguish – stealing and destroying as they wished. Macha sent her warriors to halt their destruction and they successfully vanquished all except the five sons of Díthorbae. They were to be Macha's prize. She would wreak her revenge upon them since they had failed to support her sharing in the sovereignty.

She wasn't just a powerful warrior: in the ploy she used to track them down she showed great cunning too. Disguising herself as a dirty old beggar-woman in rags, she wandered through Ireland until she traced them to their hideout in the wilds of Connacht. They were sitting around their fire and, unprepossessing though she was, they offered her food in return for sexual favours. With great coolness she agreed to their demands, requesting that she favour each of them in turn.

She went into the woods then and when the eldest came to her she overpowered him and bound him up securely. This she did with one after the other until they were all her prisoners. Then she had them brought back to Emain Macha to face their punishment. The Ulaidh required that they be executed for their shameful deeds but Macha exerted her authority with guile. She ordered them to dig the rampart of Emain Macha in preparation for her great dwelling there. In so doing she clearly divested them of their authority and indicated to her people what would happen should any of them cross her in future. It is said that she marked out the ground for them with the brooch (*eó*) from her neck (*muin*) – they had very large ornamental jewellery in those days – and so this too is offered as the derivation of *Emain Macha* (*Eómhuin*: the neck brooch of Macha).

CONOR MAC NESSA

The name of Conor Mac Nessa is familiar to much of the popula-
tion of County Armagh and has been for many hundreds of years.
Conor was the great warrior king who ruled at Emain Macha at
the time of the hero Cúchulainn. The story of how his mother came
to bear him is not quite so well known, although it is thought to go
back as far as the eighth century. He was the son of Ness, who was a
princess of the Ulaidh (the warriors of Ulster) and daughter of King
Eochaidh Yellow-heel. There is some question as to who fathered the
child Conor: there are those who say it was King Fachtna Fathach
but the most common belief is that it was Cathbhadh the Druid.
It seems that Ness was originally called 'Assa', which in English means
'docile' or 'gentle', but her name was changed to 'Niassa' which means
'ungentle' and this is why it was altered.

Ness's father, the king, had had her educated by twelve tutors and
she had proved a good student who had a great relationship with
her tutors. One night Cathbhadh the Druid and his warriors
came marauding into the area from south of Emain Macha
and in one fell swoop all of Ness's twelve teachers were killed
along with many others, and the girl turned warrior and pursued
them and because of her subsequent vengeful plundering and
destruction she became known as 'Niassa'.

At one point in her search, she left her followers preparing
a meal and set off into the wild, endlessly searching for the
killers of her people. On seeing a pool of water she abandoned
her weapons and stripped off to bathe. She was obviously
on the right trail but it proved unfortunate for her because
Cathbhadh the Druid came by and, seeing her in the water, he
got between there and her clothes and weapons and drew his
own sword. She begged mercy from him and, as was the custom
of that time, he said he would spare her on three conditions.
To agree to conditions was no mean thing in those days because

promises were binding and you broke them on peril of death. He demanded her loyalty, her friendship and that she be his wife for all time. With no means to defend herself and death her only option, she thought it better to agree. In due course she gave birth to her beautiful son Conor and Cathbhadh the Druid prophesied that he would have a great future. He was not, however, in line for kingship and the story of how he got there is one of intrigue and deception.

Some years later, when Conor was still a young boy, the King of the Ulaidh at the time, the great Fergus Mac Roich, fell head over heels in love with Ness and asked her to be his wife. What happened to her relationship with Cathbhadh we don't know – perhaps the promises she made to him were never made public and possibly the two conspired together for the sake of their son Conor – we will never know. In any case, she was loath to take Fergus for a husband. However, it occurred to her that she could turn such a liaison to the advantage of her son, so she toyed with him, saying that she would be his wife on one condition: that he allow her son to be king for a year – just for a year so that later he could say to his descendants that he had been king.

Fergus saw no threat in this and so he agreed. Ness became his wife and in due course Conor got to be king for a year. In those days kings were expected to be beautiful as well as warrior-like and Conor, who was both, was well liked. Ness, as we have seen, had perfected the art of intrigue – no doubt for her own survival. She then set about giving rich bribes to the other important warriors so that they would support Conor against Fergus and her son might retain the kingship. It worked. Fergus realised that Conor had gained great favour with everyone, and whether to keep Ness as his wife or to avoid the bloodshed necessary to regain the kingship, or perhaps both, he allowed Conor to remain as king. In spite of great conflict and internal strife among the Ulaidh, Conor maintained the kingship at Emain Macha long enough to go down in the annals for all time.

It was Conor's sister, Dechtire, who reared Cúchulainn following what was regarded as his miraculous birth. She and her husband Súaltaim, whose lands lay around present-day Dundalk, won out in the bid to foster him although, of course, it was to his uncle Conor's court that he went for his education from Cathbhadh the Druid and to learn his skills as a warrior.

Setanta Goes to Emain

This is the best-known of the stories of the Ulster warriors and children in County Armagh are weaned on it!

Before the warrior we know as Cúchulainn earned his name, he was called 'Setanta' – that was his name from birth. He lived on the plain outside Dundalk known as Muirtheimhne and he was reared by King Conor Mac Nessa's sister Dechtire, and her husband Súaltaim. As a small child, his one great wish was to go to Emain Macha to become a warrior. At that time Emain Macha was a training ground for the Ulaidh, the warriors of Ulster. Young boys came from all over Ireland to train there and it was also the residence of his uncle, the great King Conor Mac Nessa.

In preparation for the time when he would be allowed to go there, he practised with his little toy javelin every day. He played hurling with his hurling stick (the *cáman)* and ball (the *sliotar*) against imaginary opponents and he led imaginary armies into battle around his house. He had his mother tortured to let him go to his uncle's place to join the 150 boys who trained there at any one time.

'No, no,' she replied wisely. 'Perhaps when you're seven we'll allow you to go.'

But little ever stood in Setanta's way. One day he slipped off without telling anyone. It was a dangerous journey for a small boy but he had his heart set on it. He shortened the way by hitting the ball in the air with his hurling stick, throwing his toy javelin in the air, racing forward, catching the javelin and racing on to hit the ball again before it touched the ground. In this way he made light of an arduous journey.

Finally he reached a place where he could see the green at Emain Macha. This was the great playing field for the boys. He saw his uncle playing fidchell, a game like chess, overlooking the pitch where the boys were playing hurling. He became so excited that, without thinking, he ran down into their midst and got the ball from them. They, of course, were angry with this little boy for barging into the middle of their game but they were even more annoyed when they couldn't retrieve the ball from him; he just ran circles around them. They began to throw balls at him but he fended them off with his little shield. They were enraged and started to throw their hurling sticks at him. This was too much for him and his famous battle rage came upon him. He closed one eye so small that it was as tiny as a needle, the other eye he opened as wide as a bowl. He bared his teeth as wide as could be. His hair stood on end and sparks seemed to fly from the ends and the warrior moon rose from his head. He charged at the boys.

They, of course, had expected the small boy to flee from them so when they saw him come charging towards them in this terrifying state, they turned and fled. Some of them, for safety, ran round the table where Conor Mac Nessa was playing fidchell, but Setanta leapt over the table in pursuit. Conor, however, reached up and caught his arm, bringing him down.

'Why are you treating the boys in this manner?' he demanded.

'Well they haven't treated me very well,' he said. 'I came the whole way from my home to play with them and they haven't been very nice to me at all.'

'And where is it that you've come from?' asked Conor.

'I came from the plain outside Dundalk and my mother is King Conor's sister. I didn't expect to get this welcome in my uncle's place.'

'Well, did you ask the boys for their protection?' asked Conor, amused.

'Oh, no. I didn't know I had to do that,' replied Setanta.

'Well, ask them now,' said Conor.

So the matter was settled – for a short while. Before long another row had broken out and Setanta was back to see his uncle once again.

'I want the protection of the boys to be given over to me,' he stated.

'And do you think you can protect them?' asked Conor in surprise.

'Oh, yes,' said Setanta with confidence, and so the protection of the boys was given over to Setanta and there was no more fighting.

After these events it became increasingly apparent that, even though this boy was very young, he required special handling. One trait he shared with many others to this day was that he didn't like to be rudely awakened but preferred to waken naturally. On one occasion a man ventured to wake him and the boy's fist drove the man's forehead unto his brain. When Ailill, the King of Connacht, heard of the incident he commented, 'That was the fist of a warrior and the arm of a strong man!' For some strange reason no one was ever very keen to waken him after that so he was left to waken of his own accord! This is perhaps why the next event found him napping.

Once the Ulaidh, the warriors of Ulster, went into battle with a man called Eóin, son of Durthacht. It was the middle of the night and the young Setanta was still asleep and unaware of the defeat the Ulaidh were suffering until the wailing of the wounded woke him. He stretched and a witness said that his strength was such that the two stones on either side of him broke. As he gradually realised what was happening, he became alarmed and rushed out.

His mentor, the great warrior Fergus Mac Roech, was coming in. 'May your life be preserved, Papa Fergus. Where is King Conor?' asked Setanta.

But Fergus had been caught up in the heat and disarray of battle and didn't know. Setanta continued into the dark night where he met a severely wounded man who was carrying his dead brother on his back. He insisted that Setanta help him carry his brother and they came to blows over it because Setanta's main concern was for the safety of his Uncle Conor. They fought and Setanta was thrown to the ground. Then he heard the warning of Badhb, the goddess of war, saying that it was a poor warrior that is defeated by ghosts – referring to the body on his opponent's back. Stung by this, Setanta rose up and made short work of his opponent.

He called out to Conor as he searched for him and eventually received a response from a ditch. There he found the king lying amid heaps of clay like a man almost buried alive. Even though he was glad to be rescued, Conor admonished the young warrior for having put himself in danger like this.

They say that Setanta then showed the strength of six warriors in raising him up from this spot and Conor directed him to a house for shelter and had him light a fire to bring warmth back into Conor's own body. He instructed him that he might get his strength back if Setanta could catch a wild pig and roast it for him. The young warrior set off for the forest then and came across an outlaw cooking a boar on a spit. The wish to save Conor prevented the lad from being daunted by this man. He attacked him and brought the boar back. When Conor had eaten he felt the heat in his body once more and he was able, with the help of his nephew, to head for home. The young Setanta's task was not quite over, however, because on the way they met Cúscraid, Conor's son, who was also badly wounded. Setanta carried him on his back and the three reached the safety of Emain Macha. Thus Setanta proved himself to be a truly outstanding and invaluable warrior when he was but a very young boy.

On another occasion the Ulaidh were attacked by twenty-seven men from abroad. The warriors (the Ulaidh) were, of course, victims of the curse that had been put on them by Macha, so that there was no one to defend the women and boys. The strangers climbed over into the courtyard at the back of Emain Macha and the women screamed out their warning to everyone. The boys abandoned their sport and came running to the rescue, but when they saw the gruesome looking strangers they fled – all except, of course, Setanta. With a practised hand he threw stones at them and set about them with his hurling stick and managed to kill nine of them before they fled from this whippersnapper of a killing machine. He was left very badly wounded but there was great knowledge of healing herbs in those days and the cures worked very rapidly. It's worth noting, however, that a hurling stick had and still has many uses.

Cú Chulainn

One day Culann, the smith who made all the fine, ornate weapons for the Ulaidh, invited King Conor to partake of his hospitality. On these occasions Conor was always accompanied by a great band of warriors but this was to be a select gathering and so only fifty went with him! Culann's home is generally believed to have been in South Armagh on or near Slieve Gullion. It was Conor's custom to go down to the boys' playing field and get their blessing before leaving Emain Macha. This day, before he set off with his select band of warriors, he went as usual to the playing field and they watched the boys playing a game where the aim was to get a ball past all the other players and into a hole. Setanta was able to do it every time singlehandedly and yet when the others tried, he, on his own, could stop all the other players. The way he wove his way through the other boys was spectacular. They played another game rather like 'Strip Jack Naked', and one which would defi- nitely be banned nowadays. The idea in this game was to remove clothing from your opponent! In this game Setanta could strip all the other boys while they couldn't so much as get a brooch from his mantle. His feats made a deep impression on Conor and his men, and they wondered with awe what kind of warrior he would eventually become since he showed this kind of promise at such an early age. Conor decided to pay him the honour of inviting him to join the select guests at Culann's feast. However, there was still much of the young boy in Setanta and although he didn't say anything, his disappointment at having to abandon his play with the other boys was obvious. Conor, with an uncle's indulgence, told him he could finish his play and follow after them.

The Ulaidh set off and nothing but enjoyment occupied their minds. When they reached Culann's place he gave them a great welcome. After the greetings and introductions they went inside for the feast. Culann checked with Conor that his whole party was in before putting out his ferocious hound to guard his homestead and stock for the night. Candles were twinkling, musicians were tuning up and, full of high good spirits, the guests sat down to dine. So animated was the gathering that the thought of Setanta never crossed the mind of a single person there. Suddenly a great howl broke through the celebrations. It was the howl of Culann's hound and the Ulaidh froze as they remembered their young warrior Setanta. They bolted for the door and his mentor Fergus Mac Roech was first through the opening, expecting the worst. They were all utterly astonished to see Culann's hound lying dead at Setanta's feet. Fergus Mac Roech lifted Setanta high onto his shoulders with joy and they laughed at the prowess of their young protégé. Only Culann grieved for the hound: it was a great loss to him since he lived in a place where his household, as well as his lands and stock, was vulnerable to attack. He said to Setanta, 'I'm glad, boy, for your mother's sake that you are safe and well, but for my own part, I will be utterly lost without that hound. It was like the man of my house in the way it guarded us. I will be lost without it.'

'Don't worry, Culann,' replied Setanta. 'I'll rear you a hound that will be as good and until it's strong enough, I'll guard you and your stock.'

The Ulaidh laughed and said, 'You will be Cú Chulainn.'

Setanta frowned and said, 'I'd rather have my own name.' But Cathbhadh the great druid of the Ulaidh said, 'In the future, the name of Cú Chulainn will be on the lips of everyone.'

'Oh that's alright then!' said Setanta with excitement.

And from that day forward he was known a Cú Chulainn, the Hound of Culann.

CÚCHULAINN TAKES UP ARMS

This is an almost identical version of the story that I wrote for my CD 'The Cúchulainn Saga'.

It was the custom for Cathbhadh, the great druid of the Ulaidh, to instruct a hundred boys at a time in the art of druidry at Emain Macha. The seven-year-old Cúchulainn was eavesdropping one day when he was instructing the boys and Cathbhadh was asked by one of them what the omens were for that day. He replied, 'The warrior who takes up arms today will be famous throughout Ireland and stories of him will be told forever.'

When the boy heard this he ran to his Uncle Conor and said, 'Arms for me Uncle Conor!'

'Who told you to ask me that, child?' said Conor.

'My tutor Cathbhadh,' replied Cúchulainn.

Now the druids were held in great respect and Cathbhadh was the chief druid of the Ulaidh so Conor could not dismiss the matter lightly. Although he was surprised, Conor considered thoughtfully and then called for arms for the boy. A spear and shield were brought to him and Cúchulainn tested them by bending the spear, which broke; then he shook the shield and it fell apart. Another set of weapons was brought for him and it suffered the same fate. Another was brought and another. Unbelievably, he got through fifteen sets of weapons before Conor called a halt and sent for a set of his own weapons for the boy. Cúchulainn tested the spear and, mercifully, it didn't break. He rattled the shield and it remained intact.

'Happy the race and people whose king has weapons like these,' he cried.

Cathbhadh happened to be passing by and he said to Conor, 'Is that boy taking up arms?'

'He is indeed!' replied the king.

'Ill luck for his mother's son then,' said Cathbhadh.

'What do you mean?' asked Conor. 'Didn't you tell him to?'

'I did not indeed,' replied Cathbhadh.

Conor turned on the boy. 'Why did you lie to me boy?'

'It wasn't a lie really, King. I overheard Cathbhadh talking to the boys this morning so I came to you.'

'It's a good day then,' retorted Cathbhadh, 'for the warrior who takes up arms today will be great and famous and *short-lived*!'

'That's good news,' replied the undaunted Cúchulainn, 'for if I am famous, I am happy to live for one day only.'

The next morning another pupil asked Cathbhadh what the omens would be for that day. He told them that anyone who stepped into a chariot for the first time that day would be renowned throughout Ireland forever. When he heard this, Cúchulainn ran to Conor and said, 'A chariot for me Papa Conor!'

Conor sent for a chariot for the boy and Cúchulainn tested it by jumping on the shaft. Of course it broke! And several more were brought but not one of them was strong enough to withstand the strength of the boy. At last Conor said, 'Enough destruction in my house. Bring my own chariot.'

Then Conor's great chariot arrived, driven by his great charioteer Ibor, and Cúchulainn stepped into the King's chariot and this revered charioteer took him for a little turn around in it.

'Right. You can get out now, little boy,' said Ibor.

'The horses are beautiful and I'm a beautiful lad, Ibor. Take me down to the boys,' said Cúchulainn.

'What for?' asked Ibor.

'So that I might get their blessing.'

As was the custom, Cúchulainn went down to the playing fields to get the blessing of the boys. After he received their good wishes he said, 'Whip up the horses, Ibor.'

'Where to?' asked the disconcerted Ibor.

'As far as the road leads,' cried the boy.

So this great charioteer whipped up the king's pair of piebald horses and they headed for Sliabh Fuad and the lookout post of the Ulaidh. Some say the post was *Carraig an tSeabhaic* (the rock of the hawk), now known as Carrickatuke, which lies outside Newtownhamilton. Others say it was *Áth na Foraire*, the Ford of the Watching, thought to be at Silver Bridge in South Armagh. There Cúchulainn's first cousin and foster brother, the warrior Conal Cearnach, was guarding the lookout post for the Ulaidh. The great warriors took it in turn to guard this post, to make sure that no enemy entered their territory without their knowledge and to ensure the safety of visiting poets.

Conal Cearnach was very surprised, to say the least, to see his seven-year-old cousin in a chariot but as courtesy demanded he said, 'May you prosper and be victorious!'

'Why don't you go back to Emain Macha and let me guard the post?' suggested Cúchulainn.

'Oh, you could protect the poets well enough,' laughed Conal, 'but you wouldn't be fit for the fighting men.'

Now, Cúchulainn was annoyed at this slight – he was out to prove himself that day – and he took a stone and aimed it at Conal's chariot pole and broke it.

'Why did you do that?' demanded Conal angrily.

'I was just testing my shot,' replied Cúchulainn and then casually remarked,'Oh, that means you'll have to return to Emain because it's against the code of the Ulaidh to travel in a faulty chariot.'

'Even if your head is going to get left with your enemy,' said the furious Conal, 'I won't go to protect you.' And he had to return to Emain Macha and leave the boy in his stead. It was just what Cúchulainn wanted!

They went on then until they came to *Loch Eachtra* (the lake of the adventures), some say this was what is today called Lough Patrick. It is where young warriors went to demonstrate their skills. Then Ibor said, 'It's time to go home now, Cú.'

But Cúchulainn was spoiling for a fight and he wanted Ibor to continue so he tried to distract him by asking him the names of the mountains and glens.

'You may be a pleasant companion, but you're an inquisitive nuisance,' said Ibor. However, he was soon inveigled into explaining the layout of the whole region to the boy. He told him the names of the hills and valleys and the dwellings.

'And that,' he said, pointing it out, 'is the dwelling of the three sons of Nechta Schene.'

'Is it they who say they have killed more of the Ulaidh than are left alive today?' asked Cúchulainn.

'They're the very ones,' said Ibor.

'Let's go on till we meet them,' cried the young warrior.

'Oh no! Much too dangerous boy!' exclaimed the wise charioteer.

'It's not to avoid danger that we have come this far!' retorted Cúchulainn.

They went on then until they came to the fort of the three sons of Nechta Schene and there Cúchulainn tore the spancel (what horses were tied to) from the pillar and threw it into the stream. This, he knew, would be a complete provocation to the three sons of Nechta Schene. Then he got Ibor to unyoke the chariot and he lay down in it under the animal skins and said to Ibor, 'Don't waken me for one or two – just for a big crowd.'

Ibor fiddled nervously with the reigns then he yoked up the chariot because he reckoned they might just need to make a fast getaway. And this great charioteer must have wondered what madness had made him lead the chariot out of safety and into this alien territory – and all at the behest of a seven-year-old boy.

Then sure enough, out came the three sons of Nechta Schene: the warriors Foill, Fannall and Túachell.

'What's going on here?' demanded Foill.

'Oh, it's just a little boy making his first outing in a chariot,' replied Ibor placatingly.

'Well, let him take himself and his chariot and horses off this land,' announced Foill.

'Oh, we're just about to go,' said Ibor. 'You can see I have the reigns in my hand. There's no need to incur the wrath of the Ulaidh. You can see it's only a small boy.'

'It's no small boy,' said Cúchulainn, sitting up, 'but a young lad in search of combat.' Ibor's heart must have sunk.

'My pleasure,' said Foill.

'Let it be your pleasure in the ford yonder,' challenged the boy. And the three warriors went off to prepare. Ibor cautioned Cúchulainn, 'Oh Cú,' he moaned. 'What have you done? You must take heed of this first man who comes to meet you. Foill is his name. If you don't reach him with the first thrust, you won't reach him at all.'

Then Cúchulainn's *riastaire* (his battle rage) came upon him.

He closed one eye small like a needle.

He opened the other as wide as a bowl.

He bared his teeth from ear to ear.

He rose to a huge height.

His hair stood on end.

Sparks flew from it.

And the warrior moon rose from his head.

'I swear by the gods my people swear by, he will not play that trick upon the Ulaidh again when my Uncle Conor's broad-pointed spear reaches him. Mine is the hand of an enemy.'

He went to the ford and broke Foill's back with a cast of his spear, then he took his head and weapons and brought them back to Ibor.

'Right. Now Cúchulainn, take note of the next man. Fannall is his name and he treads water as lightly as does a swan or swallow.'

'I swear by the gods he will not play that trick upon the Ulaidh again. Indeed, Ibor, you have not seen me tread the pool at Emain Macha.'

Then he met Fannall at the ford and he slew him and he took his head and weapons and brought them back to Ibor.

'This last man is Túachell and understand, Cúchulainn, weapons will not fell him.'

'I swear by the gods my people swear by he will not play that trick upon the Ulaidh again for I will use the dell chliss, the spear thrusting trick. It will confuse and make a sieve out of him.' And Cúchulainn performed the dell chliss – and the man's limbs fell apart. Then he took his head and his weapons and brought them back to Ibor. Then they heard the wailing of the mother of the sons, Nechta Schene herself. And her followers were getting ready to pursue them. Ibor urged Cúchulainn to leave but his battle rage was still upon him.

'I will not abandon my spoil until we reach Emain Macha!' And when he got the heads and the weapons into the chariot he said, 'You said we'd have a good drive today, Ibor, well you'd better whip up the horses now if we're not to be caught.'

Then that great charioteer put the horses in a frenzy to match Cúchulainn's own so that they overtook the wind and the birds of the air. And when they reached Slieve Fuait Cúchulainn cried, 'What beasts are those that are so nimble?'

'Deer,' replied Ibor.

'What would the Ulaidh think it better of me to do – bring them back dead or alive.'

'All can bring them back dead but the best warriors only can bring them back alive, but you can't.'

However, Cúchulainn had Ibor whip the horses into the bog. He leaped out of the chariot and seized a fine deer and, mesmerising it, he tied it to the chariot poles so that it ran behind them as they drove on. After that they saw a flock of swans ahead.

'What would the Ulaidh think better of me to do – bring them back dead or alive?'

'Only the bravest and most accomplished warriors bring them back alive,' answered the charioteer. So Cúchulainn cast stones from his sling at the birds and stunned them. He brought them down into the chariot and while they were stunned he tied them to the sides with strings and cords so that when they revived they flew in front of it. And when they approached Emain Macha, Cúchulainn's *riastaire* was still upon him and Levarcham the satirical female poet was out on the ramparts and when she saw the chariot, she cried to those within, 'There's a warrior coming towards the fort in a chariot. There are swans flying before it and a deer running behind and he will spill the blood of everyone in the fort if naked women are not sent to meet him.'

So Conor's wife Mugain organised seventy women and three vats of cold water and when the chariot came hurtling towards the fort, seventy women with Mugain in the lead burst through the gates baring their breasts and crying, 'These are the warriors you will meet today Cúchulainn!'

And the seven-year-old Cúchulainn hid his face in embarrassment. The warriors seized him and plunged him into a vat of cold water. The vat burst and they plunged him into a second vat. Fist-sized bubbles boiled up in that one. Then they plunged him into a third and it became moderately warm. Mugain dressed him in a mantle of blue with a silver brooch and a hooded tunic. For the rest of the night he sat at Conor's knee and the Ulaidh spoke with wonder of the deeds of the seven-year-old Cúchulainn.

I was performing the Cúchulainn Saga one night for a Yarnspinning group. Since it lasts an hour and a half plus an interval, it had been agreed there would be no stories from the floor for that particular night. After the interval, however, Mealda Hall who was in her eighties at the time, went to the performance area and sat down. It was explained to her again that that night we weren't having stories from the floor because of the time factor. Mealda waved all protests aside and carried on. My heart sank as Mealda could talk for Ireland,

England, Scotland and Wales and there would be no time left to finish the saga. But my fears were allayed when this is what I heard:

There were these three fellahs goin' back to England one time. You know it was durin' the recent Troubles and all the Irish were bein' searched – especially when they got off the boat. These three men were workin' over there and they were goin' back after Christmas or the holidays or somethin'. They were travellin' by car down through Engeland and sure enough weren't they stopped by the police. The policeman leaned in and asked them all their names and the first fellah, he says, 'Cúculainn – a' course' he had to spell it out for the policeman, and the second man says, 'Conor Mac Nessa' and the next one gave his name as 'Finn Mc Cool'. Well, I think the police are still lookin' for them!

DEIRDRE AND THE SONS OF USNACH

In this story we see a much less favourable, even dishonourable side of Conor Mac Nessa. This is one of the three great sorrows of Ireland and has inspired the writers Synge, Yeats, his mentor Lady Gregory and James Stephens, and it still inspires writers today.

Feidhlimidh the Bard was feasting the Ulaidh, the warriors of Ulster. His wife, despite being heavily pregnant, spent the night pouring drinks for and greeting her guests. Late in the night, when the feast was over, she crossed the hall to retire to her bedchamber and the child in her womb screamed out. In the quiet of the night the scream was heard by many of the guests who rose up to find out what misfortune had befallen. Feidhlimidh, when his wife told him where the scream had come from, demanded an explanation from her.

'What woman knows what her womb holds?' she replied.

So they called on Cathbhadh the Druid to interpret this strange event and he said that the child in her womb was a girl. He foretold that she would grow into the most beautiful, fair-haired woman in Ulster, that men would fight jealously for her and that she would be the cause of great bloodshed and destruction. The Ulaidh were alarmed at this prediction and they thought the life of a child should not outweigh such dreadful events so they called for her to be killed.

However, Conor, the King of the Ulaidh, thought to spare her life and keep this special child for himself. Whether he had pity for Feidhlimidh and his wife and the baby or simply wanted this renowned beauty for himself we cannot be sure, but people tend to think that this ageing man had his own interests at heart. He arranged that she would live separately in a safe enclosure with only a tutor and a foster mother for company. The woman who looked after her was Conor's poetess, Levercham. Apart from the occasional visits from Conor to check on her progress and development, Deirdre (as she was named) was reared in isolation until such time as she was old enough to be his wife.

One winter's day, when snow lay thick on the ground, her tutor was skinning a calf for veal and its blood made red blotches in the snow. A raven swooped down to drink the blood and as Deirdre gazed upon the scene her girlish imagination was fired.

'Oh Levercham,' she said. 'I wish I could meet a man who looked like that: a body white as the snow, a cheek flushed red as the blood and hair black as the raven! I suppose no such man exists.'

'Oh, yes he does,' replied Levercham. 'Were you to know the three sons of Usnach – Ardan, Ainnle and Naoise – you would realise this. Why, these three men together can hold off all the warriors of Ulster. They are fleet of foot and their singing surpasses all others: it lulls men and women into peace and calm and it increases the yield of milk in the cattle. Naoise, the strongest and most beautiful, is the finest of the three.'

Deirdre's youthful heart was inflamed with this description and she thought of nothing else but to see this young man for herself.

Some say that Levercham secretly arranged the meeting and others that it happened by accident but in any case, Deirdre heard singing one day coming from beyond her enclosure. It was so fine that she figured it must be the singing of Naoise so she stole out and followed the sound until she spotted him. She walked past without looking anywhere near him.

'This is a fine young heifer passing me by!' he called out.

'Heifers will always be fine when there are no bulls about!' she countered.

Then Naoise, who had been amazed by her beauty, realised suddenly that this was the girl whom King Conor had locked up for himself.

'Ah, but you have the pick of the herd, King Conor himself,' he said.

'With the choice of an old bull like Conor and a young one like you,' said Deirdre, 'I would choose you.'

'But you can't choose me,' said Naoise, no doubt regretting the fact for the prophecy about Deirdre was well known. Now Deirdre, who had been kept from the sight of all men save the rather mature Conor and her tutor, was filled with desire for this young man who was the image of Adonis himself.

'Are you turning me down?' she cried out with indignation and when he said he was, she ran to him, held his head tightly by the ears and put a *geis* (a sacred obligation) on him to take her away with him. Then Naoise chanted loudly, a sign of danger to those in the fort, and his brothers came running to his aid.

When he explained what had happened they were alarmed. They knew that if their brother were to take Deirdre away, it would bring the wrath of Conor down on him, yet they, his brothers, could not forsake him. They decided that they must leave without delay with all their followers, so that night, under cover of darkness, they set off with 150 warriors, the same number of women and of servants. For many months they travelled round Ireland seeking sanctuary and protection in the various kingdoms

but they were so harried by Conor's warriors that rather than
cause hardship to those who protected them, they decided to go
into exile in Scotland.

When they reached Scotland, they sought protection from
no one but lived in the wild and they survived by hunting and
fishing in the glens and mountains. When food became scarce
they resorted to stealing cattle, which of course enraged those
they stole from and the latter summoned up a large force to go
against them. The Sons of Usnach saw fit at this stage to flee and
seek help from the King of Scotland.

They were given supplies and his protection in exchange for
their very considerable fighting skills. Since they were now more
exposed to the public eye, they set up their camp with great care
and had all the dwellings laid out in a circle which protected
Deirdre, whom they kept in the inner part, away from the prying
eyes of strangers. The prophecy of Cathbhadh was never far from
their minds and they greatly feared that her beauty might cause
the deaths of their men.

One morning the King of Scotland's high steward was out
early before the followers of the Sons of Usnach had begun to
stir. Out of curiosity, he wandered into their camp and, lo and
behold, he saw the still sleeping bodies of Naoise and a woman
of incredible beauty. He hurried to the King in great excitement,
telling him that he had at last come across a woman fit to be the
King's wife, that it was Naoise's woman and he urged him to kill
Naoise and seize her.

The King thought this was not an altogether honourable idea
and he told his steward that he wished him rather to go secretly
to Deirdre each day, when Naoise was away, and win her over on
his behalf. This didn't have the desired effect however; Deirdre
simply relayed the proceedings to Naoise when he came home
in the evening and so the King, in frustration, began to send the
Sons of Usnach to fight in more and more dangerous situations,
hoping to bring about their natural end in this way.

Nonetheless, the skill and daring of the warriors prevailed and so at last word reached Deirdre that the men of Scotland planned to do away with Naoise imminently. When she told Naoise they had to flee once again, he was loath to do so but she was adamant that he would not survive if he stayed another day. Their whole band left by stealth that night and set sail for an island and from there Deirdre looked back at the beautiful land of Scotland and composed a song. It told of her sorrow at leaving the lovely landscape of the glens behind and she described the places they had lived in and visited.

News of the plight of the Sons of Usnach went back to Emain Macha. When Conor Mac Nessa next held a great feast for the Ulaidh, he interrupted the proceedings to ask them if it were not true that they wanted for nothing, that there was nothing lacking in his hospitality. At this some of the warriors spoke up, saying that the Sons of Usnach were missing. They lamented the absence of such outstanding warriors and companions and decried the fact that it was Deirdre who had initiated the whole affair and not the Sons of Usnach. Conor saw that he must humour his warriors and perhaps he also saw his chance to get Deirdre back. In any case he said he would agree to their return.

Word was sent to them and the Sons of Usnach were delighted at the prospect of returning to their homeland and friends but Deirdre had misgivings. She greatly feared treachery from Conor. She told them of a dream she'd had the night before: 'Three birds came to me in my sleep,' she said. 'They came from Emain Macha and in their beaks they carried three sips of honey. They left those sips of honey with us but they carried off with them three sips of our blood.'

Ardan, Ainnle and Naoise asked that Fergus, Dubthach and Conor's son Cormac might be the guarantors of their safe return. They felt totally confident with the protection of these warriors and didn't share Deirdre's apprehension.

The wily Conor, however, had extracted a promise from the exiles that the first food they would taste in Ireland would be his, so they must come straight to Emain Macha. Then he sent for Borrach, whose home he had instructed Fergus to go to first, and ordered him to prepare a feast for Fergus and remind him that he was honour-bound to accept his hospitality. In this way he could guarantee that the Sons of Usnach would arrive at Emain Macha without Fergus's protection. Meanwhile he struck a bargain with Eoghan, son of a former enemy, that they would become allies if Eoghan would kill the Sons of Usnach for him.

Fergus was very reluctant to delay for Borrach feast but he was obliged to do so. He sent his son Fiacha in his place to give protection to Naoise and Deirdre but the couple were very unhappy about the arrangement, saying that he was deserting them for a meal. For Fergus, it was a case of being damned if he stayed or damned if he didn't and he felt sure that Fiacha would be well able to perform his duties.

After their years of exile the Sons of Usnach arrived at Emain Macha and stepped onto the green there. Conor's mercenaries were all around them. Eoghan, who had come to do the awful deed, came forward and Naoise went to meet him, but Fergus's son Fiacha, sensing some treachery, went forward to join him. As Naoise went to greet Eoghan, Eoghan greeted him with the point of his spear and broke his spine. Fiacha threw his arms about Naoise, felling him to protect him, but Eoghan finished Naoise off through the body of Fiacha, killing them both. Then they hunted Ardan and Ainnle to death like animals. Finally they tied Deirdre's hands behind her back and handed her over to Conor.

Conor's deceit bore terrible fruit. Fergus was angry at being obliged to delay with Borrach and felt dishonoured that he was prevented from staying true to his bond – to accompany Deirdre and the other exiles to Emain Macha, but when word reached him of the death of his own son as well as that of the Sons of Usnach he was frightening in his fury.

He made his way with his fellow warriors to Emain and one of them killed Conor's son and grandson. Another one killed all the young women of the province and Fergus himself killed many famous warriors. Fergus and a band of 3,000 warriors left that night and went into exile in Connacht. There they fought for Queen Maeve and her husband Ailill, although they had been no friends of theirs previously, and for sixteen years afterwards they harried Conor's men. The consequences of Conor's treachery lasted for years.

As for Deirdre, she was compelled to stay with Conor, but for the next year she never smiled or laughed. She spent her time bent over with sorrow and ate very little. When Conor brought musicians to amuse her she recited verses in praise of Naoise. When he tried to comfort her she composed a poem throwing the death of Naoise back in his face and she made it clear that she felt nothing, nor ever could feel anything, for Conor. Conor became angered by her rejection of him.

'What do you hate most?' he asked her. And she replied that she hated him more than anyone and after him Eoghan, who had killed Naoise.

'Then I'll give you to Eoghan for a year,' he retorted and he did.

The next day she travelled with both of them in a chariot to the fair at Emain Macha and she kept her eyes cast down so as not to see her two tormentors together.

'You're like a ewe between two rams,' sneered Conor.

With that, Deirdre saw a rock overhanging the road ahead and, as they galloped forward, she leaned out of the chariot so that her head might be dashed against the rock and that way she ended her torment.

And so ends the sad tale of Deirdre and the Sons of Usnach.

THE NAMING OF LOUGH NEAGH

Lough Neagh, the biggest lough in the British Isles, is bordered by four counties: Tyrone, Derry, Antrim and Armagh. The story goes that a lost

land of Ulster lies under the lough. It is a very old story which we know
was written down in the twelfth century but it may well date back
much further, some say to even the seventh century. The crux of the
story, involving a woman who neglects to attend to a well, has lasted in
the oral tradition right up to the present day.

Ecca, son of Marid Mac Carido of Munster, offended his father
grievously and was obliged to leave Munster. He set off with
his stepmother Ebliu, his brother Rib and several thousand
followers. On the advice of the druids, Rib headed west and
Ecca north. Ecca and his followers rested on the land of Angus,
son of the Dagda. He had forbidden them to stay there so by
night he had all their horses killed and threatened to kill them if
they didn't leave. Ecca protested that without their horses they
had no means to leave and Angus, with his magical powers,
produced an extremely large horse to carry all their belongings
but he warned them not to let this steed stop walking or it
would bring about their destruction.

They went on till they came to the Plain of the Grey Copse
and there they decided to settle but as they were busy unloading
the horse, they forgot about Angus's warning and a magic well
appeared at the feet of the horse which was, of course, standing
still. Ecca was alarmed by this and he had a building put up to
enclose the well and secure it and he ordered his palace to be
built nearby. A woman was then put in charge of the well and he
gave her instructions that the door to it should always be secured
except to allow people from his own palace to draw water there.

Conal Cearnach's grandson, Muridach, tried to oust these
usurpers from the land but Ecca's warriors fought valiantly and
won for themselves half of the territory and they became established there. However, Ecca's daughter was married to a man called
Curnan the Simpleton and he went around prophesying that they
would all be drowned by the overflow of the well. He declared
that his own wife, Ariu, would be among those who would be lost

but that her sister, Liban, would survive by swimming. Like many of those who prophesy, he was regarded as being ridiculous and so people paid no heed to his warning.

Unfortunately the woman whom Ecca had placed in charge of the well forgot to close the door one day and the water gushed out and spread over the ground until it had flooded the whole Plain of the Grey Copse. It was called Lough Necca after Ecca and eventually became known as Lough Neagh.

Those who didn't manage to flee were all drowned. Curnan the Simpleton died of grief at the loss of his wife Ariu. Although Ariu's sister Liban was carried off by the water, she didn't drown but, they say, lived with her lap-dog in a dwelling below the lake. She grew weary of her solitary life there and envied the fish who could travel through the water to other places and to the light. In her loneliness she cried out that she wished she were a salmon that she might swim in the company of a shoal through the lucid green waters.

No sooner were her words spoken than a transformation took place. Her body became that of a salmon but her face and breast stayed as they were and her lap-dog took the form of an otter and accompanied her everywhere. For 300 years she swam through the seas: from the time of Ecca to the time of Comhgall of Bangor, but for that we have only the word of those who wrote the story down. It seems that Comhgall of Bangor sent a monk called Beoc to Rome to speak with Pope Gregory about the rules of the Church around that time.

Beoc and his companions were travelling in a curragh when they heard beautiful singing rising from below the water. He called out, asking who sang and why, and Liban answered him, saying that she had come to arrange a meeting with him in a year's time. She asked him to bring holy men with their boats and fishing nets to this meeting so that they might rescue her from the water. Like all good requests it was met with one condition. Beoc wanted her to be buried in the same grave as himself in his monastery!

At the end of a year these holy men went to the mouth of the Larne river to meet the mermaid Liban. Once lifted out of the water, she was placed in a boat half-full of sea water so that she could swim around. People came from all over to see this woman who had such a strange shape. A young chieftain offered her his purple cloak which she declined but thanked him for his kindness and said his descendants would be known to everyone.

Then a brute of a man came and killed her lap-dog (obviously her otter had been restored to its former shape!). She lamented his loss and told the man that his tribe would be noted for their brutality and they would be weakened until they repented of their base acts. He was reduced to humility and begged her forgiveness.

Then, wouldn't you know it, these holy men began to fight over her! Comhgall of Bangor said she had been caught on his territory. Fergus said it was his net that had fished her out of the water so she should be his, and of course Beoc said she was his by right because she had promised to be buried with him. Like the good men they were, they fasted and prayed that God might send them guidance in the matter.

The decision was no less remarkable than all the other events. Lo and behold an angel appeared to them and told them that two wild oxen would come from the grave-mound of Liban's sister, Ariu. They were to yoke up a chariot to the oxen and put the mermaid into it (how she managed once out of sea water they don't tell us!) and whatever location she was taken to – there would she stay.

The next day all was done accordingly and the oxen carried Liban by chariot to Beoc's church. Before they baptised her – a foregone conclusion – they asked if she wanted to die immediately or continue her life, delaying her entry into heaven. Naturally she chose to die immediately and enter heaven on the spot. Then Comhgall baptized her and the name she was given was Murgen, which means 'sea-born' or Murgelt which is 'mermaid'. And they say that after her death she brought about miracles in Beoc's church.

THE PLAIN OF LEAFONY

Another version of how Lough Neagh was formed varies from this. It's called the Plain of Leafony or the Grey Plain. It's based on an article written in the Portadown Times *(in the 1960s) by 'The Chiel' who was the founder and owner of the same newspaper and a local historian.*

The people who lived on the Grey Plain were a magical people – wizards and the like. They lived in a *lios* or fairyfort, some called them the Tuatha Dé Danaan (the tribe of the goddess Dana). Then, they say, Clann Eochaidh came and drove them out and took over their land. This new clan settled down and reared horses, cattle and sheep but then the rivers dried up as did the wells and no water was to be found in this valley of Leafony. This, they knew, was the revenge of the wizards! There was nothing for them but to leave and find another home.

About to migrate, the tribe was stopped by a howl from the hills. It was one of the wizards. He offered them help, saying that he would make water flow for them again if they lived in peace and, crucially, they must never attempt to catch or kill any of the sacred salmon which would swim in these restored waters. The people were parched and readily agreed and even blessed him for his kindness and the wizard with his stick of hazel wandered away. Their rich life was restored to them after that. The water flowed, the pasture was green and their animals thrived.

With his newfound wealth Eochaidh decided it was time to find a mate for his daughter. A suitable match was made and preparations began for great feasting. He would put up a meal for his guests the like of which had never been seen before. He cast about for suitable food but could think of nothing quite special enough until he remembered the sacred salmon – a meal fit for the gods! He would catch those fish and serve them up to his guests at a great feast the night before the betrothal. Where the salmon had come from must be kept secret, so the night before the eve of the wedding, he went off alone, under cover of darkness, to trap the salmon. While everyone slept, he crept to the waters where these fish swam and made a great catch – no one but himself would know that the promise had been broken.

Next evening the fish were prepared and the guests arrived for the feast. The dwelling of Eochaidh was alive with talk and music and laughter but out on the plain a brooding silence reigned. The trees silenced their leaves and the heather its bells. The animals deserted the place as animals do before a tragedy and the birds silenced their song and flew away. At midnight the ominous wizard appeared on the hills above the plain and a raging torrent burst unto the valley below, sweeping everything with it in its turbulence. Wedding feast and guests, servants and followers were all devastated and the valley of the Grey Plain was sunk under water. And as this Plain of Leafony sank, there appeared in the Irish Sea its exact replica in size – the Isle of Man.

Well, that's what the legend says.

The Chase on Slieve Gullion

While many of the stories about the Warriors of Ulster have direct reference to Armagh, very few of the Fianna stories do. It would appear that Finn McCool was loath to travel so far north; however, the following is an example of one of the rare occasions on which he ventured into the mountains of South Armagh – at any rate the story says he did. It's claimed that Oisín recounted these stories to St Patrick after the former returned from Tír na nÓg (land of the forever young) following an absence of 300 years.

Culann the Smith, who made all the armour for the warriors of Ulster, had two daughters, Miluachra and Áine. One day as they strolled along the sisters talked of the man they wanted to marry; unfortunately it was the same man that they both wanted: the great Finn McCool. Now jealousy is a common enough problem among siblings and we can see that this situation might indeed lead to a few mishaps. While they were discussing their ideal man, as girls do, Áine happened to say she could never marry a man with grey hair. (P.W. Joyce, in his *Old Celtic Romances*, claims that there was a belief long ago that the water of certain wells had properties that turned hair grey while Geraldus Cambrensis states that he saw a man's hair change colour after bathing in such a well in the southern province of Munster.)

Miluachra was delighted to get this information and resolved to put it to good use. She decided that if she couldn't succeed in marrying Finn she would make sure her sister didn't either. She set off for Slieve Gullion and arranged to meet the fairy folk, the Tuatha Dé Danaan, there. She ordered them to create a lake on the top of the mountain and with druidical spells she ensured that anyone who bathed in its waters would come out with grey hair.

Not long afterwards, as Finn was walking on the green before the palace of Allen in County Kildare, a doe sprang from a thicket and bounded past him like the wind. He called his dogs Bran and Scolann and they sped after it northwards, leaving the green slopes of Allen far behind. There had been no time to call the Fianna so, with only the company of his dogs, he sped on, pursuing the doe as far north as the distant Slieve Gullion, whereupon it suddenly vanished. Finn was bewildered. How could such a thing happen? That it had escaped him after such a long chase was just incredible. He scoured one side of the mountain and his dogs searched the other.

While he was wandering around, he heard the plaintive crying of a woman and when he followed the sound he came across a young woman at the edge of a little lake, her rosy cheeks all aglow from crying. Her lips were red as berries and her neck as white as the delicate apple blossom. Her hair fell in golden ringlets round her shoulders and when she looked up tearfully at Finn her eyes glistened like stars on a frosty night.

As she paused in her weeping, Finn asked if she'd seen his hounds but she said she was preoccupied with her own troubles and, full of sorrow, she sobbed bitterly. He asked with concern what could possibly have happened to make her so distraught and offered whatever help she might request of him.

She explained that her precious gold ring had slipped from her finger and rolled down into the lake.

'If you are as strong as you appear to be, you must be one of the Fianna and then you will keep your bond of honour to help me in my distress and search until you find it.'

Though he had no inclination to, Finn at once dived into the lake and swam under water to look for the ring. After going round the lake three times he was relieved to find it. He rose from the water at the edge of the lake where the young woman sat and handed it to her. Imagine his surprise when she sprang into the lake before his eyes and disappeared.

Amazed, he stepped out of the water but as his foot touched dry land he lost all his strength and fell down, a withered, grey old man, shrunken up and trembling all over with weakness. When the hounds came up they didn't recognise their own master.

Back in the palace of Allen, the Fianna were feasting and drinking, playing chess and listening to music. Suddenly Caoilte Mac Ronan noticed Finn was missing. They became alarmed and found out eventually from one of the palace workers that he had pursued a doe northwards so they got out the hounds to pick up the scent and they set off after him.

Conan Maol, who was something of a buffoon, said he was delighted Finn was missing and that he hoped they wouldn't find him for then he himself could take his place. Although they were very anxious about Finn this made them laugh – the thought of this coward replacing their great courageous leader!

Their search took them to Slieve Gullion on top of which they came across a shrivelled old man lying beside a lake. At first they thought it might be a fisherman but from the wrinkled skin hanging off his bones they thought his poor state was caused more by sickness and neglect than old age. He didn't answer them when they enquired if he had seen Finn but lay there shaking all over and then seemed full of grief, uttering feeble cries and wringing his hands. Even when they threatened him he wouldn't answer but lamented all the more. At last he beckoned to Caoilte Mac Ronan and whispered to him what had happened. He, in turn, reported it to the others and they set up such a hue and cry in their anger and alarm that the foxes and badgers rushed with fright from their dens in the hollows of the mountain.

Then Conan Maol threatened Finn, wielding his sword and showing delight in his downfall. He reviled the rest of the Fianna and cast up to them how Finn's father Cumhal had been killed by the Clann Morna. He wished that all the Clann Baskin were reduced to Finn's state and said he would make short work of laying them low.

It was Goll Mac Morna who had killed Cumhal and taken over leadership of the Fianna in a great fight between the Clann Baskin and the Clann Morna, but when the young Finn came of age he won back the leadership of the Fianna. Conan was, of course, a member of the Clann Morna and though he had sworn allegiance to Finn there was lingering resentment there.

Finn's son, Oscar, scorned him at first but Conan taunted him with cowardice and Oscar rushed at him. The cowardly Conan ran from him and begged the Fianna to protect him. Peace was made.

They then set off, carrying Finn on a makeshift stretcher, and made for the fairy palace on Slieve Gullion, for they knew Miluachra lived somewhere in a cave below it. Once there, they all began to dig that they might find her and force her to restore their leader. They dug for three days and three nights till at last in her cave she heard the dreadful noise they were making and when they broke through her walls, she saw their vengeful looks. She had a potion that could restore Finn but she was reluctant to give it to him. However, when she saw his graceful young son Oscar she was filled with admiration for him. Her heart thus melted, she gave the red-gold drinking horn to Finn.

He was instantly restored to his former shape when he drank from it – all, that is, except his hair, which was now a silvery grey. Though Miluachra was willing to restore that too, everyone thought the soft silvery hue of his hair so fine that he decided to keep it like that.

After three of the warriors had drunk from the wisdom of the horn it gave a sudden twist and, entering the loose earth at their feet, it sank out of sight. A growth of slender twigs grew from that spot and that area of bushes is thought to contain the wisdom of the drinking horn because, if you look on it first thing in the morning while fasting, you will know in that moment all the things that will happen that day.

So that's how Finn's hair was changed in one day from golden yellow to silvery grey.

Now that you know the story you might be able to understand and enjoy this local, colloquial version of it, called 'Finn McCool and the Cailleach Bhiorra' (*cailleach*: witch, crone; *biorrach*: sharp, tricky person).

The Cailleach Bhiorra lived above on the top of Slieve Gullion and she was a witch, and she could turn herself into anything when she wanted to go through the country. She used to turn herself into a deer or a stag and Finn would be out hunting and would chase the stag and was never fit to catch it. And he had a great pack of dogs and the best of them was one they called Bran.

He used to rise this deer near Mullacrew and it would run like the wind down through The Gap of the North here and into the bushes – this country in South Armagh was all bushes then – and that'd be the last Finn would see of it.

So he laid some sort of a trap this day. And when they riz the stag he managed to turn it, and as far as it was told the stag had to run up through Ravensdale and Annaverna and up the mountain and Finn's dog Bran on its heels. Finn followed it as hard as he could, and here he comes on Bran – stone dead: maybe that's where they buried him, at Carnamadda on Ravensdale mountain.

But Finn tracked the deer some way or other and away up Slieve Gullion and he lost the track up there. He come as far as the lake on Slieve Gullion, and here was this hellishin fine looking young woman sitting on one of thon mill-stones that's above at the lake, and her crying like the rain. Finn didn't know her from Adam.

He asked her what she was crying for, and she said she'd lost this ring; whether she said she was married or single I don't mind [remember], but this was an awful valuable ring and she'd be foothering [fumbling] with it and it dropped into the lake.

So he asked her where and she told him, and without another word in goes Finn into the lake and dives down, but damned the sight of ring or thing could he see, and he was more than lucky to be able to swim up and out: and when he come out he was a done old man and his hair was as white as snow. There was no sign of the fine young woman, but only this old cailleach of a one and her laughing her length at him: it was The Cailleach Bhiorra all the time – she'd changed herself into a young woman. She was fed up with Finn chasing her and now he was hardly fit to stand. So she seen Finn's men coming and she dives into the lake herself and that was that. Finn's men come up and didn't know a bit of him, only one of Finn's dogs run and leapt and smelled around him and when Finn told his story they knew he was telling the truth.

'The job then was what were they to do? But some one of them advised them what to do: to dig down alongside the lake and hoke the Cailleach out. But when they started to dig it was all solid rock. So they had to go back apiece, and back apiece, and had to keep going back till they come to where the Cailleach Bhiorra's House [a chambered cairn on the summit of Slieve Gullion] is the day, and they were fit to dig down there. And they sort of made a tunnel with big flags as they went until they were right up agin the lough and ready to drive a bar through.

And then the Cailleach herself come up and shouted at them to stop, or the lake would flood through the hole and drown Ireland. So they made her give back Finn his youth again and she did, but she wasn't fit to change the colour of his hair.

And from that day till the day he died Finn McCool had white hair.

(Michael J. Murphy's *Now You're Talking* (Blackstaff Press), p. 107)

Not a Man at All

There's a story told about the wife of Finn McCool, the all-powerful leader of the Fianna. A much stronger man (alternatively a Scottish or Danish giant) was coming to fight him. With a female's quick-wittedness, she decided to hide him in a large cradle, covering his head with a frilly cap and pretending he was her young child. When the other brute of a man comes to the house looking for Finn she deceives him with her talk of how Finn is off hunting and of how powerful he is. She gives him bread full of stones and gets him to put his finger in the 'baby's' mouth to check that he is developing teeth. Nursing his badly bitten finger, he decides that it's not wise to take on Finn McCool if even his huge baby is so vicious and he leaves hurriedly.

The following is a version which T.G.F. Paterson, the curator of Armagh Museum, collected in South Armagh:

Finn, I may tell ye, wusn't the only pebble on the beach in the early days. An' if even all ye hear is true, but then it's not – for half the truth is downright lies when it comes till giants an' sich like – well then Finn wusn't half the man some people think. Indeed he wusn't much of a man at all! Shure there's not a sowl [soul] from here till Newry that doesn't know that Finn hid in a cradle once rather than take hes batin' like a man. An' for days before he had been struttin' the mountain as proud as a paycock, pretendin' he was blue moulded for the want of a fight.

An' this is the way of it. Finn wus on the hill above when he saw a giant the spit of himself, but a far bigger man restin', tween the two oul' teeth (two craggy hills) on Carrick beyant [beyond]. An' he didn't like the look of him at all, at all. So he in till his wife an' says he, 'I'll be murdered completely if thon fella sees me.'

'Finn,' says she, 'leave it till me,' an' with that she makes a cradle of sorts. An' then she had a look over till Carrick herself an' there wus the other one footin' it over. An' troth an' she got a fright at the size of him. Says she till herself, 'I've mebbe bit off more than

I'll chew,' says she, 'but what's till be, will be,' says she. 'I've done me best an' I can't do more.' An' before ye'd say 'God save ye,' the other fellow wus with her.

'Good morrow, me woman,' says he, 'an' where is hes self?'

'Och,' says she, 'he's jist stepped out this minit for a walk till the Kerry mountains (hundreds of miles away), but it's back he'll be in a little while,' says she.

An' what with that he spied the cradle. 'An' hat have we here?' says he.

'Och,' says she, 'that's our youngest chile, but as ye can see for yourself he is but an ill-thriven brat.' 'Shure,' says she, 'me ouldest one's worth lookin' at, but it's out with hes father he is.'

An' that wus enough for the other fella. Says he, 'I'll call again some other day, for I can't be waitin' no longer now.'

And he ups an' away an' off he goes over mountain an' bog but divil the back he iver come till Slew Gullion (Slieve Gullion mountain).

An' that's Finn for ye! An' shure the men are the same till this blessed day – always blowin' and blastin'.

(T.G.F. Paterson, *Country Cracks*
(Dundalgan Press, 1939), p. 24)

The Navan Dragon

This tale about Emain Macha, based on an account by T.G.F. Paterson in Country Cracks *(p. 45), is very different in tone and much more fantastical than the other tales associated with the site.*

It was said that if you didn't bear the blood of the rightful owner you could not partake of the treasure trove that lay under the still waters of the lake at the Navan Fort. And who would know that you weren't the rightful owner? A ferocious dragon that lived under those deceptively still waters.

Old O'Rourke had seen it for himself while out mowing in the field that ran down to the lake. He was working away when he heard a strange kind of sound, something like a cross between a screech and a whistle – not a pleasant sound at all. He had his back to the lake at the time and it gave him a fright. He turned round and near fell in when he saw a terrible ugly looking head, oh an awful thing, sinking down in the middle of the lake. O'Rourke had never seen the likes of it in all his born days, the whole lake was trembling with big waves coming running out to the edge. The hair rose up on his head and he took to his heels and fled. It'd be a while before he went back there.

It was seen at the King's Stables too in the townland of Tray. Isn't it a good job the Kings of Ulster aren't still waterin' and washin' their horses there now? They've always claimed that there's a class of a passage goin' from the lake over to the stables – underground like. You know O'Toole? Well, would you credit it, he started diggin' into the mound – the mound! Tryin' to drain the land, he said. Well he didn't keep that caper up long for out slithered a long slimy lookin' baste – a snakey class of a customer. It rose up forninst him renderin' everthin' dark and O'Toole near turned t' stone. But he tuk it all in just the same: the big, bulgy eyes, he says, were pokin' out at him tryin' to fix him to the spot. He still can't remember how he come to again. But the wife says he come home and tuk to the bed. I tell you, he's not the better of it yet.

The Camlough Dragon

It seems, though, that there were a lot of dragons about in those days. Paterson heard about one in Camlough. This is my version of the one Paterson recorded (p. 46).

Take the one in Camlough. I suppose it lived in the lake there. Well, Finn McCool met it one day and you can't imagine what it was like. Now if I say to you that it was as big as a mountain you'll have some idea; of course the mountains in County Armagh aren't as big maybe as mountains in other places but they're big enough for a dragon. His head was as big as Sturgan at the north-west end of Camlough lake and that's 864ft high. But worst of all was his mouth: it was lying open and full of teeth and them the size of trees. As for its tail, it went so high up in the air that you couldn't see the end of it. Knocking over a man or a cow would be no bother to that tail!

Do you think Finn McCool was scared of it? No way! Of course he had his whole band of Fianna with him and if they weren't fit for a whole fleet of dragons, I'll eat my hat or whatever comes handy. Be that as it may, the dragon swallowed Finn and then it swallowed the whole of the Fianna, every man Jack of them. But of course that was no obstacle to Finn, for he was quare and handy. He just took his sword and slit its belly and the men hopped out one by one. The brute was so put out – whether from the slit in its belly or the fact that they got away I'm not sure – that it lay down, there and then, and died. You know there could still be dragons in the lake at Camlough.

THE BLACK PIG'S DYKE

The Black Pig's Dyke is an earthwork which was built to block the gaps in the drumlins that provided a natural defence and cut off the north from the rest of Ireland up to the end of the sixteenth century. It runs through a number of counties all along the border of old Ulster. The bank is about 30ft wide and 20ft deep. In some counties the rampart has been levelled for top soil and the people are no longer aware of its existence. Several parts, like the Dorsey (doirse: doors) in South Armagh, are still recognisable. It's thought that these 'doors' were one of the main entrances to the north at the time of King Conor Mac Nessa. Some say that Conal Cearnach's son Miann built the dyke to keep the Connacht men from entering Ulster, others that it marked the boundaries of provincial kings in early Ireland or simply that it helped to prevent cattle raiding.

The story is told that a local man noticed that his son was greatly 'failed'. He went off to school every day with the others in the family and never claimed to be sick but he was getting thinner and thinner by the day and seemed tired all the time. He finally asked his son if there was some problem. Why was it, he asked, that he seemed to be wasting away, especially since he was eating the same food as his brothers and sisters and they were all thriving.

Then the boy revealed that the master was performing some sort of ritual on them every day.

'The master puts us into different shapes. He makes me a hare and the others hounds and they run after me. Every day he turns me into a hare and every day the others try to run me to ground. I'm dead beat and heart scared of them catching me. Afterwards he uses this big book that he says has great powers and, with this, he turns us back to our usual selves every evening.'

His father was angered by this account but all he said to the son was, 'I'll go to the school tomorrow and have a word with him.'

He spent some time thinking about how he could get the better of this man of learning and he went to the school the next day and said to the teacher, 'Is it true you have great powers and can do these things I hear about?'

When the master replied that he could, the father challenged him, 'Change yourself into a pig then and let me see for myself.'

So there and then the master turned himself into a pig, but the father was just as quick for he had figured out in his mind beforehand what he would do. He took the book and quickly put it into the schoolhouse fire. Squeal though he might in the form of a pig, the master couldn't get it from him, and of course he needed the book to be able to turn back into his human form again. The father stood over the fire while the book burned and a difficult job he had keeping the pig away from it.

As the book went up in smoke, the pig lost his senses altogether and he ran through the country, tearing up the land as he went. He had a huge horn growing out of his snout and people were too terrified to go near this wild pig. Eventually, somewhere in the neighbourhood of Tullaghan, it ran into the sea and was drowned, though there are those who say that when it came within sight of the sea, it turned off in a different direction.

It must have had incredible stamina because the Black Pig's Dyke runs from near Donegal to County Armagh and some would say becomes the Dane's Cast in County Down!

Sometimes in the accounts of this incident it's the mother who changes the master into a pig but yet another version of the story says that a magic fog fell on the people, and men on horses saved themselves by going underground at Ardee in County Louth. In doing so, they escaped drowning but to this day they are accompanied by the pig, and the pig will one day rise up and run on the ground. This will waken the men and they'll follow it to a great fight at the river Dee and the river will run red with blood. They claim that local people have gone down there and seen the men asleep on their horses and that the pig was there too. The story has at times been connected to the prophecy that there will be war or great slaughter in the valley of the Black Pig. This war is alternatively the destruction of Ireland and the end of the world.

So, there you are: we have all that to look forward to!

The number three crops up frequently in versions of the story: the pig has been said to have *three* legs; one side would lose the war after *three* days' fighting and there were *three* rows of poison sticks at the Black Pig's Dyke to deter the enemy from entering the territory.

This story is found all around the area of the Black Pig's Dyke: South Armagh, Monaghan, north Cavan, Meath, Westmeath and north Leitrim. Strange sightings have taken place from time to time along it. A farmer whose poor land lay along the Dyke reported coming home one evening and seeing a black man walking along the Dyke on the opposite side to himself. This would have been an extremely rare sight in those days. One dreads to think of some destitute fugitive, trying to eke out an existence in the bogs of Ireland.

Another man said that, as a boy of seven, he and some friends had pooled their money to buy a pack of cards. They took it in turns to keep them for the night so they'd all have their fair share of them. One night he was coming across the Dyke with the cards in his pocket and he crossed into a field where the hay was all made up in small stooks. As he entered the field a sudden, strong wind blew through it, scattering the hay and tossing the boy about. The cards fell out of his pocket onto the ground but he was so scared by the sudden gust that he didn't stop to pick them up; he just took to his heels instead. The next day, as he came back through the field again, he saw that the hay was once more sitting neatly bound up and his cards were there too. The cards, though, were cut up with the diamonds cut out and placed on some whole cards and likewise the clubs, spades and hearts. These destructive gusts of wind that arise without warning were quite common and were known as 'fairy winds'. In fact, there's a meteorological explanation for them – but not for what happened to the cards!

On another occasion, in 1918, a girl of about twelve saw a black pig with six piglets. She told her schoolteacher about it and described how it was acting strangely. The teacher went to look but could see nothing. However, two of the little girl's friends claimed to see it too and later on another girl as well. No one else could see it but the girls insisted it was there and that it was always in the same place. In fact the children were alarmed when the adults went too close; they said the pig was crossing over their feet.

Two men in that locality had cut down a tree in a fairy fort and had become ill and, of course, the two events were perceived to be connected and people flocked to the spot to see if they could see the pigs. Though no adults actually saw them, some reported that they heard the pig move and grunt. It caused a great stir at the time and the newspapers were full of it.

At the time of writing there have been no recent sightings!

THE DEATH OF FERGUS MAC LEIDE

The following story, originally written in medieval Irish, can be taken as a satire on the warriors of Ulster. Despite the title, the story is really

*about the experience of Iubdan, King of the Lepra and Lepracan
(midgets and tiny midgets), when he visits Emain Macha.*

King Iubdan was a noble and stately king renowned for his
nobility and great standing. His palace and raiment were beyond
compare and he ruled over a goodly people. Many and notable
were the courtiers of his court and great were the offices they
held. This great king held a great banquet and among his noted
warriors in attendance was Rigbeg (*beag* means 'small' in Gaelic)
son of Robeg, Luigin son of Luiged, Glunan son of Gabarn, Febal
son of Feornin, Brigbeg son of Buan, Liran son of Luan, Mether
son of Mintan and their poet Esirt son of Beg, son of Buaidgen.

Their strong man too was there, he who could perform the
great feat of cutting down a thistle with a single stroke and he who
could not be thrown by fewer than ten men. As was the custom,
the guests were all seated in order of importance. On one side of
the king sat his wife, Bebo, and on the other his chief poet, Esirt.
Great was the celebration and merriment induced by the drink
from the wooden red vats. It was poured by the pourers and the
meat was carved by the carvers and the music of their mirth rose
to the rafters. With his drink in his hand, the great King Iubdan
arose and greeted his guests, 'Have you ever seen a king that was
better than myself?'

'We have not!' they cried.

'Have you ever seen a strong man better than my strong man?'

'We have not,' they replied.

'Have you ever seen men of battle better than those who are in
this house tonight?'

'Indeed we have not!' they declared.

'I tell you now, it would be a hard task to overcome or take
captive any of the valiant warriors here this night. They are what
kings are made of.'

Then the chief poet laughed and King Iubdan of Lepra and
Leprechaun said, 'Oh why do you laugh, my chief poet Esirt?'

'Because, sire, I know of a band of warriors one of whom could perform those tasks on all our warriors.'

'Lay hold of him!' cried the king, 'and let him be punished for such treachery!'

Esirt was duly seized but protested that this act would have poor consequences, that the king himself would be in Emain Macha for five years and would escape only by leaving behind one of his great treasures.

'Give me but three days and three nights to travel to the great house of Fergus son of Leide. If I don't manage to bring back something that will prove the truth of my words then do what you will with me,' said Esirt.

He was released and then Esirt, chief poet of Iubdan, King of Lepra and Leprechaun, donned his fine silk garments of red and gold. He wore his little gold-decorated bronze shoes and he took with him his white bronze poet's wand, which he shook when he finally reached the gates of Emain Macha. The gate-keeper of that great palace eventually discovered that the sound had been produced by a tiny but beautiful little man standing knee-deep in the grass.

All this he reported to the Ulaidh, the warriors of Ulster, who enquired if he might be smaller than their own dwarf poet, Aed, who could stand on a warrior's hand. The gate-keeper assured them that this diminutive man could stand on Aed's hand. They roared with laughter and curiosity and Esirt was brought before them but, addressing the huge men around him, he asked if the smallest of them might deal with him since even he would be deemed of formidable height in his own country.

So he was brought in to their feast, balanced on Aed's hand and the king, Fergus Mac Leide, offered him a drink. Esirt refused this hospitality and since this gave insult to the king, Fergus suggested that he be dropped into the drink, which the cup-bearer duly did. The stately little man floated on the surface and from this vantage point he appealed to them all as poets of

Ulster, saying that he had great knowledge to impart to them
and would they really let him drown?

He was then rescued and made dry again with satin and
silk clothes. He proceeded to prove his powers to the king by
revealing that he, the king, was dallying with his steward's wife;
that his own foster son had eyes for Fergus's wife, the queen,
and then he flattered him by reassuring him that many fine,
cultured women found the king attractive above all others. With
Fergus's permission, he declaimed a poem about his own King
Iubdan of Lepra and Leprechaun. The warriors were so pleased
with his poetry that they heaped gifts on him but he refused
them, saying that everyone where he came from had riches
enough. The warriors were honour-bound not to take the gifts
back so he suggested they divide them between themselves and
the poorer in their land.

After three days and three nights Esirt set off for his own
country accompanied by Aed, the poet, who had volunteered
to go with him. When they reached the sea Aed wondered how
he would cross it but Esirt assured him that King Iubdan's horse
would bear them over the waves. Then Aed saw a hare with a
bright red mane approaching them through the foam. It had four
green legs and a long, drifting, curly tail and its bridle glittered
gold and its eyes flashed fiercely. Aed was loathe to mount such
a creature but Esirt reassured him and the two sped across the
waves on the steed of Iubdan, King of Lepra and Leprechaun.

When they arrived they were greeted with much surprise
and awe at the 'giant' Aed, but Esirt explained to Iubdan
that this 'giant' was but a small man to all the others of his
country and could stand on the hand of any of their warriors.
Then Esirt put a *geis*, a sacred obligation, on Iubdan that
he go to visit Emain Macha and be the first to try the king's
porridge, which was made nightly. This obligation, which he
could not fail to comply with, filled Iubdan with dread and
he consulted with his wife Bebo, asking that she accompany

him. She reminded him that had he not seized Esirt in the first place, he would not now find himself in the position of having to visit these giants.

However, the two set off and managed to enter Emain Macha unobserved. In the kitchen they even found the large pot of porridge, which Iubdan could only reach on horseback it was so far up. Then disaster befell him when he tried to balance on the edge of the pot and reach down to the silver spoon to taste it; he slipped and fell in while his bewildered wife Bebo waited below for him. Finally she called out to him, 'O dark man, and O dark man!' She addressed him this way because of his jet black hair and his lily white skin – save for the cheeks red as forest berries. Since all the people of Lepra were fair he alone had the distinction of being dark. She went on to urge him to make great haste.

'O fair-haired woman, and O woman of the fair hair!' he replied – and that because she had fair hair. He went on to describe the sticky mess he had got himself into and ended by selflessly urging her to flee and save herself, saying he would be in that place, exiled, for a year and a day.

Great was the hilarity when Iubdan was discovered in the porridge pot and he was carried to Fergus Mac Leide for his perusal. The ignominy of it! Fergus observed that, though tiny in stature, he was not the same colouring as Esirt the poet had been. He addressed him as 'wee man' and sought his identity and then ordered him to be well guarded and put among the common people. Iubdan protested that the foul breath of these people offended him and he gave his word not to try to escape. (In those days people had a high regard for honour: their word was their bond and were they to break it, it could mean death.)

So Fergus permitted him to stay amid the warriors and Iubdan often sang them verses of poetry – as was the custom of the time for all cultured men and women. He prophesied the death of some of Fergus's men and these came to pass and he reproached others for thinking they could dictate their own fate.

Then seven battalions of the Lepra and Leprechaun came to bargain for their king. They offered to flourish Fergus's kingdom with corn. When Fergus refused to release Iubdan they had the cows sucked dry – to no avail. They contaminated the water – to no avail. They destroyed the mill beams and kilns – to no avail. They ruined the corn crop – to no avail. Then they threatened to shave the hair off the women and men and Fergus said that if they did that he would kill their king. But Iubdan reproached his battalions then and told them to make good the damage they had done and make their way homeward without him. They left then, grieving in poetry which is, of course, a very effective way of grieving, and they would feign have put a poetic curse on Fergus were it not for the disapproval of their good King of Lepra and Leprechaun.

At the end of a year Iubdan sought to fulfil Esirt's prophecy and offered a choice of his great treasures to Fergus in exchange for his freedom. He offered him his spear, his shield, his sword, his cloak, his shirt, his helmet, his tunic, his cauldron, his vat, his mace, his horse-rod, his timpan, his shears, his needle, his swine, his halter, his shoes, and he sang the praises of each of these treasures in turn. He urged Fergus to choose one of them but as fate would have it, this was the time that the poet Aed returned from his sojourn in Iubdan's country and he sang a lay of its praises. Finally, and not before time, Fergus chose Iubdan's shoes in exchange for the little king's freedom and off he went and glad he was to go. The warriors of Ulster, however, were filled with sorrow at his parting.

And now unfolds the story of the shoes. King Fergus went bathing with a friend one day in Loch Rudraige. The monster of the lake, 'The Stormy One', became aware of their presence and, shaking the waters into huge waves, she rose up, towering like the arc of a rainbow. Then she pursued the men, who were swimming for their lives to reach the shore. As fortune would have it she caught up with Iubdan just before he reached dry ground. She breathed her foul monster breath upon him and he became crooked and distorted. His eyes squinted and his mouth was twisted round to the back of his head. Worst of all was the fact that he had no idea of what had happened and he looked so hideous that none dared ask him how the change had come about and all the mirrors in his house were hidden.

The truth will out, however, and his companion came home and told all to his wife who in turn informed Fergus's wife. One day when she and Fergus were having an argument as to who would use the bath first, Fergus flew into a rage and hit her, breaking her tooth. This was too much for her to bear and she said he would be better to take out his rage on the monster of the loch that had distorted his face, instead of on a poor woman. Of course he didn't understand the truth of her words till she confronted him with a mirror and great and terrible was his amazement at what he saw.

He assembled the warriors of the province then. They gathered around him in their ships upon Loch Rudraige. Once more the monster reared her fearsome head to a height of three times 50ft. At her rising the ships were overturned and the men floundered. But the brave Fergus bade his men stay safe while he tackled this great monster single-handedly wearing the shoes of Iubdan, King of Lepra and Leprechaun. He strode stately of stature upon the waters of the loch and the hideous tough-skinned monster rose and bared her fangs at his coming. She arose from where her body formed, as it were, a great hill, and from that great height she bared these terrible teeth and Fergus looked into her foul, gaping mouth rather than the deep-set vicious eyes. Three fifties of clawed flippers she was furnished with on both her sides as she bent her neck towards her foe. Fergus surged forward, crying out in poetry how he was fulfilling the prophecy. They grappled then in the lake so that the very fish were evicted from the waters and the banks became rich beds of salmon. The milk-white water of the loch turned to a red foam with the blood of the battle. Then the beast turned and Fergus pursued it, his wounds spurting, until he killed it with his famous great sword, the best in Ireland.

Then he took the heart from this dreadful dragon and brought it back to the warriors, but his body had as many tooth marks as a sieve and he had as many wounds as the monster. When he tried to speak he spurted blood until, at last, he managed to spout poetry instead and chanted how he had wrought revenge on the dragon at the request of his wife, how Iubdan's shoes had brought him through undrowned and how he would rather die than live misshapen.

Then the great King Fergus Mac Leide declared that his death was upon him and he asked the warriors to take his special sword and preserve it for a great warrior that would come after him, one Fergus Mac Roech. Then he bade them all farewell and died.

Thus endeth the sad tale of the gold-ornamented, white-bronze shoes, treasure of Iubdan King of Lepra and Leprechaun, and how they carried Fergus Mac Leide across Loch Rudraige to his fatal wounding.

2

THINGS RELIGIOUS
AND IRRELIGIOUS

Armagh is the ecclesiastical capital of Ireland. It appears to
have been a religious centre down through the ages and has had
significance not only for Christians but for the pre-Christian
era as well. The early Christians in Ireland very cleverly incor-
porated much of the native religion and customs into the form
of Christianity they taught, and their Christianity was consid-
erably different from that taught later.

It was generally thought that the Navan Fort (*Emain Macha*),
was the dwelling of Conor Mac Nessa and the Red Branch
knights (the *Craobh Rua*) in the Iron Age but there has been a
great deal of controversy over this. When archaeologists were
excavating the site, they came upon what they deduced to be
a ceremonial structure. It was a limestone cairn within a 40m
wooden structure and they concluded that it was used for
some type of religious ritual. Whether it was because the area
had religious significance or because it was a seat of political
power, or a little of both, St Patrick decided to build a church
in Armagh.

The Bull's Track

There's a hardly credible yet oft-told story about the first church St Patrick built. Perhaps it was to explain the mark of a bull's hoof in the ground at Ballymacnab: a townland 7 miles outside Armagh City where today there is a junction of two roads beside a church. The track seems to have been there for centuries – perhaps through the ages – and it's known as the Bull's Track or the Bull's Foot.

The story goes that St Patrick tried to build his church at Armaghbreague (this comes from the Gaelic meaning 'false Armagh'). The men worked at the building every day, and every night a bull would come and knock it down. St Patrick tried to tackle the bull with the support of the local people but the bull rampaged through the countryside for miles around. It leaped from one site to another, leaving the mark of its hoof in several places the best known of which is at Ballymacnab. It has been suggested that the bull represented the hostility of the local pagan population to this new 'Christianity'.

The following version of that story was collected in South Armagh and appears on p.99 of Michael J. Murphy's Now You're Talking … *(Blackstaff Press, 1975). It mentions Oisín, who was one of the more famous members of the Fianna and grandson to Fionn Mac Cumhail (Finn son of Cumhal).*

The time St Patrick met Oisín and converted him, Oisín had turned into a very old man; and St Patrick was building his church at Armagh at the time.

But he was getting no further with the work; every blessed night this bull would come out of the woods and cowp [overturn] and scatter all they had built during the day.

Patrick was beat. And in the latter end he said his only remedy was to ask Oisín if he could do anything about this wild bull: Oisín was a giant of a man you understand, a powerful man altogether in his days with Finn and the Fianna, before he went to Tír na n-Óg [The Land of Youth].

Well, Oisín good enough heard the story, and he allowed he thought he'd be fit for the bull if only St Patrick would pray for him to have the strength of twenty men of that day.

St Patrick said he would, and away he goes to pray for Oisín to get the strength of the twenty men, and the Lord heard his prayer and Oisín got the strength of the twenty men of that day.

But it was no good: the bull came that night after Oisín bet [beat] it away and knocked and scattered what they'd built that day the same as usual.

So Oisín asked St Patrick to pray that he might have his old strength back again. And St Patrick went away and he prayed hard, and Oisín's former strength was given back to him, restored, the same as it was before he went to Tír na n-Óg.

And that night he faced the bull again; and it was a long hard fight and in the end an – dammit he mastered the bull and the Divil's own fight he had to kill it.

But before Oisín killed the bull it seen it was at last meeting its match and when it could do no more it give a lep [leap], a wild lep at Armaghbreague, and the track of its hooves is to be seen in the rock of the mountain there to this day.

Oisín killed the bull, but he was done out. So he skinned the bull and put the hide about him like a cloak and made his way back to where St Patrick had the masons building his church. He was that far through [exhausted] he could go no further, so he lay down with the hide of the bull about him, and in no time he was sound asleep.

The following morning early St Patrick's men come again to start at the building of the church: and there was Oisín, as sound as the bells, asleep and snoring.

Then St Patrick come up and he seen what had happened and Oisín asleep. He told the men for to creep up and by all and any means take the cloak off Oisín: he was afeared what might happen if Oisín awoke and the power still on him.

So they crept up. Oisín was still snoring; and he sucked the men up to him, and when he snored out with every breath he pushed them back again; in and out. And St Patrick seen it and the men, Oisín's snores sucking them in, his breath blowing them out: in and out, in and out.

There was only one thing he could do. He went away to pray; and if he prayed hard the first time for Oisín to get back his strength to beat the bull he prayed twice and three times as hard for the Lord to take the strength away from Oisín while he slept, for God only knows what notion Oisín might take into his head when he'd waken.

And St Patrick's prayer was heard.

Well be that as it may, in most versions of the story the bull was successful in destroying the church which was being built on Armaghbreague and the bull was en route to Emain Macha when he left his track on the ground. In any case, St Patrick was still on a mission to find a bull-free zone where he might build his church.

SALLY HILL

Around AD 445 St Patrick sought permission from Dáire, a wealthy local chieftain, to site his church on Druim Saileach (Hill of the Sallies or Willows). Dáire, however, refused him. He did allow him, though, to site it far below, near the bottom of that hill in what today is Scotch Street. It was called Teampall Na Fearta (Church of the Holy Relics). It subsequently became a monastery and then a convent until the dissolution of religious houses in the sixteenth century. In the recent past it was the site of the Bank of Ireland and today it's a home for the elderly called St Patrick's Fold.

According to tradition, St Patrick's sister, Lupita, was buried there. Indeed, in the early days the body of a female was exhumed. It had been buried in a vertical position with two crosses: one in front of and the other behind the body. The surmise was that it was Lupita but there was no evidence for that. In 1633, according to James Stuart's *History of Armagh*, another body was exhumed. It was that of a woman and the body was still intact; however, when 'profane hands' touched the body, it disintegrated. Many believed that the miraculously preserved body proved that this had been Lupita.

Patrick was persistent in his crusade to obtain Sally Hill and he visited Dáire's house often. There's a story told about one of Dáire's servants allowing his horse to graze on the ground Patrick had been given for his church. Patrick protested to him but he was ignored and the horse was left there overnight. When the servant came for his horse next morning it was lying dead, so he rushed off to report this offence to Dáire, who was furious and ordered Patrick to be killed.

No sooner had the man left to carry out his wishes, than Dáire himself was struck down and his wife said it was because of the power of Patrick. She cancelled Dáire's order to kill him and instead made a plea for him to restore her husband. Patrick is supposed to have blessed some water and told the servant to sprinkle it on the horse, which revived on the spot. Then some was sprinkled on Dáire, where it had a similar effect.

Dáire was so impressed by his powers and no doubt grateful at having his life restored, that he sent Patrick a gift of an extremely large and beautiful bronze cauldron. Patrick's response was, 'Let me give thanks.'

Dáire, eager to know what impression his ostentatious gift had made, asked the messenger what the Christian had said when he received it. When he heard what the reply was he was disappointed and then plain angry. 'If that's all he has to say, go and take it back again,' he instructed the same messenger. When the man explained to Patrick that he was taking away the cauldron, Patrick's response was again, 'Let me give thanks.'

On hearing this unexpected reaction, Dáire declared that Patrick was very consistent and therefore a steadfast man; so impressed was he that he decided to give him back the cauldron and he delivered it personally this time. In addition, he offered Patrick the land he had sought all along for his church: Sally Hill.

Patrick always made it clear that he received his special power from his God. In restoring people from the dead his reputation and that of his God grew and it's suggested that Dáire was baptised a Christian in the end.

Although there may well have been a chieftain Dáire, Dáithí Ó hÓgáin in *The Sacred Isle* (p. 189) points out that 'Dáire' means 'the fertile one' and that it sounds more like a reference to the Daghdha – one of the Irish pre-Christian gods who did indeed possess a wonderful cauldron and was renowned for his generosity. Ó hÓgáin suggests that this fits very well with Dáire's gifting of land.

The Book of Armagh, written around AD 807, tells us that when Patrick was formally marking out the site for the church with bell and book and accompanied by both companions and curious onlookers, he disturbed a doe with a fawn lying in the undergrowth of the willow trees.

'Here,' he said, pointing to the spot where the deer had lain, 'shall God's altar stand.'

The startled doe fled but when Patrick lifted the fawn gently and carried it down the hill, the fawn returned and followed meekly behind him. He crossed the small valley and placed the doe on the slope of the neighbouring hill Tealach na Licc (Sandy Hill). This is generally accepted as a prophetic reference by Patrick to the building in his honour of the present-day Catholic church: St Patrick's Cathedral some 1,400 years later.

So Patrick built his church on Sally Hill and other buildings grew up around it like the Culdee monastery, the Abbey of St Peter and Paul in today's Abbey Street and Teampail Bríd

(Brigit's Temple) in Chapel Lane until the city became a seat of learning with students coming from far and near. At one time there were 7,000 in attendance.

It's believed that the remains of the High King Brian Boru are buried on the north side of the Old Cathedral because his last wish on the battlefield of Clontarf in 1014 was, 'My soul to God and my body to Armagh.' He is reputed to have previously rested in Armagh for a week and left a 20oz-collar of gold as a gift to the Church – but as you might expect the gold has disappeared. He also wrote in the Book of Armagh and of that there *is* evidence.

The Cathedral was burnt and plundered many times by the Danes and fabulous treasures were stolen from it. It was wrecked at the time of the Restoration but in spite of being destroyed and rebuilt many times through the centuries, what is now the Church of Ireland Cathedral, also known as the 'Old Cathedral', still stands at the heart of Armagh today. It faces the Catholic Cathedral and for many people these two, visible for miles, are what make the city distinctive.

The Catholic Cathedral was built on Sandy Hill at the foot of which Patrick had placed the little fawn, so in some ways the two are connected. The building started in 1840 but the Great Famine intervened, with all the death and destitution that that involved, and so the building work was halted for a while and it took nearly fifty years to complete. It was finished in the early 1900s. Considering the contentious past of the two religions, there seems to be more cooperation than competition between them nowadays.

Another treasure in Armagh was St Patrick's Bell and the eleventh-century silver-gilt casing for it. It was commissioned by the King of Ireland in the twelfth century. The back is silver plated but the front is encrusted with rock crystals. The design is of elongated beasts intertwined with snakes. The bell and shrine were entrusted to the care of the Mulholland family until the

last keeper died in the nineteenth century. The shrine eventually found sanctuary in the National Museum in Dublin.

HOLY WELLS

St Moninne's Well

Holy Wells abound in Ireland; it's estimated that there are over 2,000. These wells were important sites of pilgrimage in Ireland long ago and they appear to have maintained a spiritual significance since Pagan times. There are still pilgrimages today to a small number of the many Holy Wells but of course the practices have been Christianised.

County Armagh, like most other counties, has its fair share of them though some are better known than others. This is usually because people have recorded practices and cures connected to the wells.

Michael J. Murphy described the annual pattern to St Moninne's Well in Killeavy in his novel Mountainy Crack. *Killeavy is in South Armagh and St Moninne (AD 435-518) decided to spend her latter days there. She was also known by many other names: Blathnad, Blinne, Darerca. It's said that she was baptised by St Patrick when he made a visit to her parents. Her father, Mochta, was a local king, and her mother was the daughter of a king. The well lies above the ruin of an old church and for many years there was a very popular pilgrimage to it.*

It is recorded that some time after Moninne's death they were building a monastery in Killeavey and they needed one very large piece of wood for a crucial part of the structure. After some searching they came across a really large tree trunk which they succeeded in cutting down for the job. However, it proved utterly impossible to move, no matter how they tried. The account states that the abbess prayed earnestly for guidance and, lo and behold, the next day they found the large trunk in an open space near where it was needed. Not only had no one moved it but they could find absolutely no sign that it had been moved. They scoured the ground for a trail or at least damaged bushes or growth, but none was found. When they looked at the trees around the direction from which it must have come, they noticed that there were signs of broken branches at the top of some of the trees and they could only conclude that it had travelled through the air!

St Patrick's Well
People are keen to continue visiting a well and spreading news of it if a miracle cure is recorded as a result of drinking or using the well water, or if its reputation has been handed down through the generations. Such a well is to be found in the Leger Hill area, on the outskirts of Armagh City. The road there is considered to be part of an

ancient route between the hill where the Old Cathedral now stands
and Navan Fort (Emain Macha). It also lies close to the Old Callan
Bridge – famously captured by the painter John Luke. The High King
of Ireland, Niall Caille, drowned in the Callan River in AD *846.*
St Patrick's Well lies near that spot but has sadly fallen into decay and
disuse but in former days it had great importance and people flocked
to it. In the booklet Of Other Days Around Us, *Patricia Kennedy*
recounts how she visited it as a child with her mother:

I remember my mother bringing me out by the hand and I was
only a child. And she swore by it. And I remember us tying a wee
rag on the thorn bush and kneeling down. And the horses and
the carts up Leger Hill – you couldn't have got moving for them.
They came from all over the countryside: farmers, farmers' wives,
because they believed there was a cure in it for animals as well, you
know. And everybody brought bottles and things like that with
them. And I remember one year we had a scorching, scorching
summer and I remember going out and my mother telling me to
kneel down and I looked in and it was just totally cracked, dried
earth. That's all it was. And I remember even as a child thinking
to myself there couldn't be any water coming there, you know. But
I remember on the stroke of midnight – we were all kneeling round
the well – and this wee trickle came through just like a dampness
into the earth and then more and more and more and that's how
that well filled up. Now I witnessed that. I would only have been
about seven or eight years old and I witnessed that. And I've never,
ever forgotten it. Because even I, at that age, was saying to myself,
'There's no way water could get through there.' But funny enough
it did. And I remember the farmers and all coming over. My mother
had a bottle with her, and she put the bottle in – that's how much
of it there was at the finish up – she put her bottle in and filled it;
so did everybody that was gathered round the well and I remember
the farmers coming over and taking water in bottles too for their
children and their animals as well. It was always just called the Night

of the Well; it was the 28th of June on the stroke of midnight going
into the 29th – that's when it sprang because my daughter's birthday
is then and my mother always used to say, 'She was born on the
Night of the Well'. I always remember the date.

St Mochua's Well

St Mochua's Well is in the townland of Derrynoose outside
Keady. There were a number of St Mochuas but this particular
one is said to have had a military career and to have become a
Christian cleric at the age of thirty. He lived and founded religious
establishments in other places before retiring, like St Moninne, to
County Armagh. St Mochua went to Derrynoose, where he died
in AD 657 at the age of ninety.

There's a story told that the well used to be on the opposite side
of the road. Then one day a man came along with his horses and
let them drink in the holy well. The well water disappeared to the
great consternation of the people in the area, who had revered
it for many years. They were shocked at what they regarded as
his desecration of the well and prayed for its restoration. To the
amazement of all, the well rose again on the opposite side of the
road where it stands today.

The water has the reputation of curing eye complaints. Some
say there's no spring to the well yet it has never run dry, even in
times of drought. 'St Mochua's Well' is actually signposted on the
road in a number of places but the well itself, though it has a sign,
lies inconspicuously behind a hedge but bears all the marks of
having regular visitors.

It's interesting how the Pagan and the Christian practices
intermingled: the Holy Well was also called a Wishing Well and
it had a stone that was used specifically for that purpose. They say
that if the stone was turned clockwise between sunset and sunrise
it could prove a cure for anything and everything, but if turned
anticlockwise it brought misfortune. Apparently at St Mochua's

Well there was a particular stone that was said to be used to inflict curses on people, hence the expression 'praying prayers on someone', which was used in the locality as a euphemism for wishing someone harm. The practice was taken sufficiently seriously for a local priest to order the stone to be removed and buried because it had been so effective in bringing ill luck to people. He chose two men, in whom he had great trust, to raise the stone at night and bury it in darkness in a place that they would never reveal to anyone. It's said that the two men went to their graves without breathing a word of its whereabouts.

St Brigid's Well

St Brigid's Well, in Armagh City, has recently been restored. It lies near the golf course in a tract of land where the ruins of the thirteenth-century Franciscan friary are to be found. No doubt there were many stories connected with it in the past but they seem to have been lost because for many years it lay forgotten and in disrepair – much as St Patrick's Well is now. Most of Brigid's life was spent in other counties but, like Mochua, she came to Armagh in her later years. It must have been a veritable Bournemouth for the sainted community!

PRAYING PRAYERS

A Toast to the Turnip

An ecclesiastical event took place at Castledillon, a stately home just outside Armagh City. The Molyneux family had bought over the land when the Dillons were no longer able to maintain it. Paterson gives an account of it in his book *Harvest Home*. He lists the eminent scientists and scholars in the Molyneux family one of whom wrote a radical pamphlet that so incensed the authorities that they had it burnt in public. Through succession the title became Sir Capel rather than Molyneux. The Sir Capel in residence towards the end of the eighteenth century was regarded as extremely eccentric; he was in favour of Catholic emancipation yet he was a strong Williamite and he was a very keen violinist, though by all accounts he played appallingly!

He made great use of the wonderful setting of his house and estate for throwing lavish parties. These included dancing, feasting and boating on the lake, with one particular party lasting two days and two nights. On that occasion there was a concert on the second night and for this he had an orchestra present. The players were greatly alarmed when they found that he was absolutely set on being leader of the orchestra. Now, apart from his lack of skill, his violin was often out of tune; it would have been disastrous. The night was saved when some genius had the idea of soaping his bow so that, although he fiddled to his heart's content, no sound came out but, with the swell of the orchestra all around him, he didn't realise that he wasn't contributing to it!

However, the laugh was not always on him; he could turn the tables and managed to do it very deftly on one occasion. On the appointment of Archbishop Stuart as Primate of All Ireland in 1800, Sir Capel very generously threw a celebration party for him. He invited guests that he thought would be mutually interesting to the parties involved. The archbishop, who is said to have equalled Sir Capel in eccentricity, decided not to go at the last minute. It's difficult to understand how he could do such a thing since he had accepted the invitation, but in any case he sent his chaplain in his place and, to add insult to injury, he sent with him the gift of a huge turnip. While it may have been the pride of his vegetable garden it wasn't exactly the most elegant of gifts for such a lavish party.

Apparently Sir Capel received the turnip from the chaplain without comment but when they were all seated for dinner they found that the turnip had been placed in the seat of honour that had been reserved for the archbishop. Sir Capel then proceeded to drink a toast to the turnip and gave a most eloquent and learned speech – addressed to and about the turnip – stopping occasionally to consult it on the finer shades of ecclesiastical or intellectual matters. This resulted in great hilarity among the guests but the poor chaplain was mortified. One wonders what report he gave of the proceedings to the archbishop.

A very different attitude to ecclesiastical personages is recorded in situations like the following:

During a deluge a priest under his umbrella rushed into a low thatched house where an old man and woman lived. They had never seen an umbrella before. The priest left down the umbrella to drip inside the door. They chatted, the shower passed and brilliant sunshine came out; the priest left to go, forgetting his umbrella.

When he had gone the old couple saw the umbrella. They were unable to get it through the narrow door. In the end the old man ran after the priest and called to him, 'Father? You forgot your wee house and we can't get it out the door.'

The priest returned, let down the umbrella, and left. The old man says to his wife, 'See that? Isn't the power of the priest great?'

(Michael J. Murphy, *Now You're Talking* ... (1975), p. 12)

Pope's Hill

In spite of its wonderful ecclesiastical lineage, Armagh is by no means without healthy irreverence. A cousin of mine lived near a place known locally as Pope's Hill, which is out in the country-side. When he was growing up he always assumed that the hill was named respectfully after the Pope. He never bothered to enquire about it because he instinctively knew it must be connected to religion and have some sort of 'holy' significance.

As an adult he discovered that in a previous generation a man who lived locally had a habit of getting very drunk in the local pub, which was perhaps a mile away. As he made his way home across the fields in the dark – no doubt staggering and taking the odd tumble – he was heard to curse the Pope with great venom and fluency and so the place became known as Pope's Hill!

For the Good of Her Ass
When material gain was only to be had if you practised a specific religion, some people decided against martyrdom and took a pragmatic approach, like the woman in this story that Michael J. Murphy got from his father:

During the Great Famine when proselytism was fairly rife, a minister approached an old woman to change her religion. He had found her grazing her donkey along the road. In return he agreed to afford her grazing for her donkey on the lands of The Glebe.

A few Sundays later the parson noticed the old woman leaving the Roman Catholic church following Mass, and then later she attended his own service. He reproved her for this dualism of devotion and asked her to explain her conduct. She replied, 'Your reverence, I go to Mass first for the good of my soul, and then to your service for the good of me ass.'

(Michael J. Murphy, *Now You're Talking* … (1975), pp. 12-13)

'A Bag of Begods'
Religious practice in Ireland has had many interpretations and misinterpretations, as illustrated by another anecdote that Michael J. Murphy collected from Myles Mallon in County Armagh:

There was another fellow not quite as bad as the last and it seems he went to the same priest; or one like him. He was making his Confession anyhow and said he had two main sins to confess. So the priest asked him how many times he had committed these sins since his last Confession. The fellow said he didn't know.

'You'll have to know,' says the priest, 'or I can't give you Absolution. What do you work at?'

'I'm a plough-man for the landlord,' says he.

'Have you any sacks in the field?' asks the priest.

He was no way short of bags and sacks.

'Well,' says the priest, 'when you find you've committed one of those sins put a wee stone in one sack; and when you find you've committed one of the other sins put a wee stone in another sack. Come back next Saturday night.'

Saturday night come. Well, in them times the chapel for Confession would be lit with a few candles: two at the door, on every side aisle, and maybe two near the altar rails. The chapel was full anyway when the priest heard this woeful commotion, someone banging and staggering agin the seats like a drunk man. He put his head out of the Confession-box to demand what was wrong, and here he sees this fellow with a full bag like a sack of priddies [potatoes] on his back. He dumped the bag down agin the confession-box and says he:

'It's only me, Father. There's the bag of Begods an' Be-Jazes. I have the other bag of whore's getts out in an ass's cart at the gate.'

(Michael J. Murphy, *Now You're Talking ...* (1975), pp. 4-5)

Derrynoose

I had the pleasure of talking to Paddy Corrigan in Derrynoose recently. He is in his nineties and has great recall. He said that in his day he was more interested in dancing than storytelling and somehow that gave more credence to what he had to say. He told me about a friend of his and his account went something like this.

Early one May morning the friend was going to market with a few cows when he saw a couple of men coming down the slope of a field. They held a rope between them and they walked at some distance apart – each one with an end of the rope in his hand – and as they walked the rope brushed the grass between them. At first he wondered what they were doing and then he remembered it was the first day of May and that dew collected on a May morning had special qualities. Certain words had to be said with the collection of it depending on what charm the person wanted to activate, but it was often a malicious request, as it was in this case, where they wanted the wealth of that particular farm to come to them instead of to the owner.

He was curious because he'd often heard of these happenings and he idly wondered if there was anything to them or if they were just 'old superstitions'. A typical phrase used in the charm would be 'All to me', meaning that all the milk, butter or wealth of the land should come to the person saying the phrase. So this man, as a light-hearted experiment, said 'And half to me' and on he went to the market and thought no more of it. In the following weeks his cows began to give so much milk – more than he could ever use – that he became alarmed. He thought better of having taken part in what, he decided now, was a practice that couldn't be right at all. He became so troubled by it that he went to the canon (high-ranking priest) to ask for advice and no doubt he was advised to make some kind of amends to the farmer whose cows must have been left giving little or no milk. After that experience he didn't ever dare take part again in any of the May morning activities.

These charms were frequently used around the milking of cows and the making of butter in a churn. There are many accounts of such practices. It seems that the charms were very successful in stealing away a neighbour's milk or butter. The thefts were a type of curse that was put on the farm and they were, and in some places still are, described as 'praying prayers' on someone. What an ironic title for something that usually has a suggestion of malice about it. I'm reliably informed that it was common practice. Of course there were charms that could be sought that would undo the curse; in the past there were people who had all this kind of knowledge. The person who had had 'prayers prayed on them' would go along to the wise man or woman to seek a remedy for it. For instance, the remedy for a cow's milk yield being reduced or having disappeared altogether was to get a strip of clothing from the person who had wished the milk away and burn it under the nose of the cow. Christianity tried to root out all these practices and has been largely successful, but only in the last sixty or so years.

There's one custom, or some might say superstition, that's still observed in many parts. If you had a 'lone bush' in the field you gave it the beestings. The beestings referred to the first milk a cow gave after calving and it was poured into the ground around what was known as the Fairy Thorn or Tree. This tree, or 'lone bush', was a hawthorn tree and it often stood alone because there was a taboo against cutting it down and although a field might be cleared of all other trees this one would be left standing, even if it was right in the middle of the field. The same applied if the tree was blown down or knocked down, people wouldn't touch it but instead let it wither away. It was used though for May Morning. They used to cut a branch and stick it into the dung heap in a farmyard and hang various little things from it and this was to bring good luck to the farm and its inhabitants. In another instance a man was cutting branches to stop cattle hurting themselves as they capered about the fields. He cut a few hawthorn branches and thought he heard a moan but he carried on until blood came from the gash. He was so alarmed he tied them back up with splinters and in a few days time they had grafted well.

My elderly friend told me about another way people had of 'praying prayers'. 'People would take a grudge against one another for very little reason in the past,' he said, 'and they would pray prayers on one another.' These 'prayers' often consisted of saying that no one of the family you bore a grudge against (in other words no one of that name), would ever live on the land again, or for a specific number of generations. He mentioned two local families and said that that had happened to them and that it had come true. The heir of one farm had died young after an accident and the person who inherited the other farm had emigrated and didn't want the land in Ireland so he sold it. Therefore the malicious wish had come true in a way, but then, accidents happen all the time and people often emigrate for life so who's to know the validity of these things.

Cart in the Kitchen

Of course 'praying prayers' was only a small part of the story and Phil Mohan, an eighty-year-old man in the same townland, told me something of the high-jinx they used to get up to. 'Well,' he said, 'there was no television or computers like nowadays so, as young fellahs, we were always looking for something to do, some way of playing a trick on, or torturing, our neighbours!' They had a neighbour who would go to market with his donkey and cart and when he sold whatever goods he had he would go for a drink with a friend or perhaps he would clinch a deal in the pub over the sale of an animal.

The local lads would watch out for him coming home a little the worse for wear on the donkey and cart. They waited till they were sure he would be safely in bed and snoring a little drunkenly and then they would dismantle his cart (this wasn't very difficult to do). As no one locked their houses in those days, they quietly entered the kitchen and reassembled the cart inside and the *coup de force* was when they took the donkey inside and hooked it up to the cart.

When the poor man awoke in the morning with, no doubt, a sore head, you can imagine his consternation when he saw his donkey and cart in the kitchen. The most bewildering thing of all for him was how he had managed to drive it in there the night before.

I've heard of this happening in various places and if the man was married and he had come home after his wife had gone to bed, we can just imagine the telling off he received in the morning!

Stray Paths

The Fairy Path
This story also came from Derrynoose though it crops up in many parts of Ireland. It was told to me by a young girl in Derrynoose Primary School. She got it from one of her grandparents.

A farmer is coming home late one night and when he is quite near his house, he crosses one of his own fields and for some very strange reason he can't find the way out of it. He goes around the field keeping to the ditch but no matter how much he tries to find it, the exit eludes him. Now, this is a field he knows like the back of his hand so he can't understand it at all. He wanders round and round his own field for what seems like hours and eventually he gives up and lies down on the damp grass and tries to sleep. In the morning, the way out of the field is perfectly clear in the early light. It's a tired and bedraggled farmer who enters the house for breakfast.

His mother upbraids him when he tells her the strange thing that happened to him. Did he not know he was on the Stray Path? If you stray unto the Fairy Path, she says, you could be lost for hours or even longer. Didn't he remember they had to check the site before they built the house to make sure a Stray Path didn't run through it? Did he not remember how often, when they had company in, the talk had been about it and what the remedy was if you were lost on it? You take off your overcoat or jacket and you turn it inside out, pulling the sleeves through as well. Then you put it on again – inside out and you're right as rain. You'll find the way out no bother!

So the next time I'm lost in the countryside driving around and around in the car and despairing of ever finding my way because of diversions, I'm going to get out of the car, take off my jacket and ...

The Hungry Grass

Another child in the same primary school told the story of the hungry grass. It's also referred to by the folklorist Michael J. Murphy when he was writing about the Slieve Gullion area in *Mountainy Crack*. If people, young or old, were out walking on land that wasn't their own, they had to be very careful not to walk on the hungry grass. It was claimed that there were incidents of people dying of hunger in some particular spots. It was such a firm belief long ago that youths were advised to take slices of bread with them if they went out for a day's sport, and to always keep a slice in their pocket. If they found themselves on the hungry grass – and they'd know because they'd become weak and eventually completely fatigued by hunger – they should just take a bite of bread and they'd revive.

Some people believed that famine victims were buried under these places and that those who stood on the ground were somehow experiencing the fatal hunger of some of the million who died and, indeed, were buried in random places during the famine of 1845-8. Older people didn't talk much about that event. They hadn't been told a great deal about it by their parents who had experienced it. In the past silence was a common way of dealing with a national tragedy.

3

OUTLAWS

REDMOND O'HANLON

I found T.W. Moody's Redmond O'Hanlon *(1937) and John J. Marshall's* Irish Tories Raparees & Robbers *(1927) very useful for information and stories about O'Hanlon.*

During the seventeenth century, the Gaelic aristocracy and gentry in Ireland were dispossessed of their lands. They were well educated and skilled swordsmen but had no means of livelihood so they took to the woods, which covered most of Ireland at that period, and became virtual highwaymen. They naturally engendered great loyalty in the common people who had been their former faithful tenants. These people they never harmed or robbed but they caused great problems for the authorities. The result of this was, of course, that they were relentlessly pursued. This gave rise to the word 'Tory', the Gaelic *tor* meaning pursuit; *tóraí* subsequently came to mean 'outlaw' or 'bandit'.

Redmond O'Hanlon, born in 1640, was a notorious Tory (*tóraí* in Gaelic). In the past, an O'Hanlon had been chieftain of an area which included South Armagh and extended beyond it and the

O'Hanlon clan owned a considerable amount of land before they fell into disfavour with the English authorities. Redmond was said to have been educated in England and so had an excellent command of the English language as well as his native Gaelic.

When he found himself in danger of being caught for his Robin Hood-like activities it's thought that he fled to France – hence his military skills and his fluent French. He returned to continue his activities and when things became too hot for him in one area he moved to another. Throughout Ireland he was both greatly esteemed and feared, depending on which side you were on. He was said to have had a band of about fifty followers and was regarded as their captain. This band guaranteed protection to the farmers for a small fee and those who were no friends of his dared not travel without a convoy or without the 'say-so' of O'Hanlon. He inspired tremendous loyalty among both his comrades and the common people and was known as the Count or Captain O'Hanlon. The ruses with which he tricked his unfortunate opponents were legendary and he gained both fame and infamy. He was described as 'a most accomplished gentleman, equal to Ossory, who was accounted for manners and bearing the finest cavalier since Sir Philip Sydney'. It was also said of him that he was an 'excellent actor and mimic, able to impersonate a king's officer, merchant or countryman …'.

No One Robs in My Name

One day, while riding ahead of the rest of his troop, he came across a pedlar who was lamenting the loss of £5 (a great amount of money at that time) and his box. He was cursing one Redmond O'Hanlon who had stolen them. Then he described how he had tried to hold on to the box and this Redmond O'Hanlon had knocked him down, kicked him and abused him like a dog. This didn't please O'Hanlon too well, as it was not his style at all. He swore at him and made it clear that he'd never seen the wronged man before.

By this time his fellow Tories had caught up with him and, having got a description of the thief and an idea of what direction he had gone, they all set off to apprehend him, leaving the bewildered but chastened old man behind. When O'Hanlon returned with box, money and thief, the pedlar must have thought him a good angel! However, O'Hanlon insisted that the pedlar prosecute the real thief at the next assizes. He wanted to teach the robber or any like-minded robbers a lesson so that they wouldn't dare rob again in his name.

O'Hanlon wrote a mittimus and sent the criminal, under guard, to Armagh Gaol. The robber's counsel managed to get the trial postponed but the whole thing was a great source of amusement to the judges and everyone in the court. There was great hilarity at the idea of O'Hanlon (the highwayman) acting as a Justice of the Peace.

In 1674, a proclamation for his arrest was made. Around that time he became very ill with a fever. For some time he lost the use of his limbs but his friends cared for him, moving him from place to place, out of harm's way and they collected for him his protection money, which the vast majority of the people were willing to continue paying even though he was, of necessity, inactive. The danger to him was such at this time that they had to move him south and he was eventually caught. His comrades came to his aid once again, rescuing him when he was on his way to the gaol in Naas.

In 1676 another proclamation went out to bring him in, dead or alive. His escapades were so ingenious, however, that they won the (no doubt grudging) respect of the authorities. The following is a good example of his tactics.

'Count' O'Hanlon's Military Escort

He went to Armagh City disguised as a country gentleman, put up at the best inn, and asked the commanding officer if he would let him have a military escort as he needed protection when crossing the Fews (the hilly area of South Armagh). He told him that he was carrying a considerable amount of money and was afraid of meeting Redmond O'Hanlon!

His request was granted on condition that he give the men a little money first, which he duly did – a very generous amount. They travelled a number of miles and then he announced that he was now out of danger and that they could return – their duty was over. He gave them some more money and ordered them to charge and fire their rifles many times in celebration of the excellent job they had done in giving him safe passage. When he figured they had used up all their ammunition, he whistled to his comrades who rose from the ditches around and stripped the soldiers of their arms, money, clothes and belongings and he ordered them to return to the city – without their uniforms!

His activities obliged the government to station a military troop in the area. These soldiers hounded O'Hanlon, trying to corner him. He resented their relentlessness so much that he wanted to get his own back.

Horse Rustler?

When a new unit took over, O'Hanlon saw his opportunity and perhaps he wanted to warn them off. He took eighteen of his men and when the soldiers were sleeping he spirited away eighteen of their horses. Next morning a party of thirty-six soldiers set out to follow the tracks. They caught up with the Tories but O'Hanlon spotted them before they reached him and he formed a half moon shape with his men – every one of whom stood close to his horse. This meant that the military wouldn't fire in case they wounded the horses. There followed a stand-off until O'Hanlon thought best to make them an offer. He anticipated that they might try to reach the ground behind him and so put his band of outlaws at a disadvantage.

He proposed that the military pay a guinea a piece for their own horses and that they allow the Tories to get away unharmed, otherwise, he declared, they would fight to the bitter end. A parlez was held and the whole thing was agreed and carried out so that the mission was accomplished without a single shot. As usual, O'Hanlon departed with his bag of money!

Someone did get the better of him though and, surprisingly enough, it was a young apprentice:

Many a time Redmond O'Hanlon held up a coach on the road over at the Gap of the North and only himself in it [alone], and it'd be guarded with soldiers. He'd have heads of cabbage in the hedge and hats on them and let on they were his men. But a wee servant boy in Dundalk tricked him.

This lad was hired with a big Dundalk merchant and the merchant had to collect a debt in gold in Newry, but he was afeared of O'Hanlon robbing him. No one would face to go for fear of Redmond. And the wee servant boy said he would go.

'Good man,' says the merchant, 'and I'll get you the fastest horse in the stable.'

'Oh I don't want the fastest horse,' says the wee codger, 'but give me the worse old horse you can lay your hands on. And I'll want no pistol.'

Well, they couldn't understand why he wanted an old done slow horse and he wouldn't tell them. But he guaranteed the merchant that he'd have the gold back with him safe and sound.

'I'll see and make it worth your while,' says the merchant. 'It's a bargain.'

Off the wee codger sets sail on the old horse. And of course somewhere half-way he meets this fine looking gentleman, well dressed and riding a very fine horse.

'Good day, me boy,' says the gentleman.

'Good day, sir,' says the boy.

'Where are you going?' asks the gentleman.

'I'm going as far as Newry,' says the boy, 'to lift a debt in gold for my master but I'm heart afeared of meeting Redmond O'Hanlon.'

'Don't be one bit afeared,' says the gentleman. 'I'll be here when you're coming back and I'll see you come to no harm.'

And of course who hell was it only Redmond O'Hanlon himself.

Well, the boy rode on and one way and another reached Newry and got the debt in gold in a wee sack or satchel. But he changed one of the sovereigns and said he wanted it all in small coppers. Ties it. He puts the satchel of sovereigns in under the saddle and hangs the sack of coppers on the saddle. Mounts up and away back for Dundalk.

Well, when he come to the place – there was a wood there along the road – here he meets the same gentleman sitting waiting on his fine horse.

'Well,' says he, 'did you do your job?'

'I did,' says the boy.

'And where's the gold?'

'I have it here with me,' says the boy.

'Then,' says Redmond, 'your money or your life. I'm Redmond O'Hanlon. Hand it over.'

'Well,' says the boy, 'I never believed in handing money to anyone in my life. Go and pick it up.'

And he whipped the bag of coppers off the saddle and fires it well into the wood. Redmond laughed and got down off his fine horse and away into the wood to get the sack, and then off with the servant off his old horse, leaps on Redmond's fine horse, and away galloping like mad for Dundalk. And of course Redmond hadn't a hope in hell of overtaking and catching him on the old horse.

(Michael J. Murphy, *Now You're Talking* … (1975), p. 55-7)

O'Hanlon was known for his kindness to the poor and for this reason as well as the fact that he was regarded as a true gentleman, no one betrayed him, although there was a considerable price on his head. It's notable that he counted among his friends both Scots and English, though, of course, not among those he harried. For those who suffered at his hands, however, it was becoming a matter of some urgency that he be caught. In 1680 there was the sum of £100 being offered for his head. And 'his head' was not a figurative expression in those days. It wasn't only kings who were beheaded; they literally cut the heads of the dead Tories and brought them to the authorities to demand their prize – a kind of 'Cash on Delivery' service. It had become imperative to catch and kill O'Hanlon and serious measures were taken to carry it out.

The Boat Trip

A Captain Trevor Lloyd was given free reign to do so and soldiers were put at his disposal. Having 'scented' Redmond they drove him down to the shore of Carlingford Lough. With no retreat possible into the path of so many soldiers and with no way forward, O'Hanlon was thrown back on his wits. He told a boatman that he was ill and had been advised by a doctor to go out to sea. If this boatman would row him out there would be a good chance he could empty his stomach through seasickness and bring about a cure. More to the point, he would give the boatman the princely sum of ten shillings, which was the equivalent of a week's wages for the few hours involved. This won the boatman over and they set off.

When they were a short distance from the shore O'Hanlon looked back and saw numerous soldiers making their way towards the shore. Afraid that they might manage to pursue him in another boat, he spoke hurriedly to the rower, asking him to make his way to the other side of the headland. The owner was loathe to do this as he might get blown off course by winds but when the Tory produced his pistol and told him he would never make land again if he didn't, he became more compliant. O'Hanlon then plied himself to the oars to speed matters and they managed to get out of the sight of the pursuers. They rowed back and forth, keeping out of sight until night fell, and they entered a creek under cover of darkness. The Tory paid the man well for his pains and made his way by paths and backroads to a safe house.

There are many stories about O'Hanlon's escapades but the historical evidence is limited, though this doesn't necessarily mean that the tales handed down are not true. We may never know. The authorities had perfected the art of turning Tory against Tory: by giving one man his freedom and often a cash prize for delivering the head of another or at least informing on him. And this is how the ending of Redmond O'Hanlon's short, but oh so eventful life was brought about. The authority to arrange his downfall was ultimately divested in William Lucas, who received a command in the army as a reward. Lucas got Redmond's follower and foster brother Art O'Hanlon on board. Art took advantage of the fact that he was keeping watch while O'Hanlon slept and he shot him. One account says that he shot him and fled and when another look out, William O'Shiel, came into the hut Redmond, who was not yet dead, asked him to take his head when he died and prevent the authorities from obtaining it. According to this account O'Shiel did carry out his wishes but troops were sent out on a search and eventually the head was found. It was impaled on Downpatrick Gaol in County Down.

So after many years of great loyalty from his comrades he was betrayed at the heels of the hunt. Tradition has it that his body is buried in a graveyard at Ballynabrack on the road from Tandragee to Scarva. Another tradition says that it is in Relicarn, an old graveyard in the townland of Terryhoogan.

The fifteenth generation of a branch of the O'Hanlon clann is still living in Mullach Bán in South Armagh. The present dwelling is a public house and has probably been a tavern for hundreds of years. Part of the site dates back to the early 1700s. Some say that O'Neill camped here on his way from the Battle of the Yellow Ford to the Battle of Kinsale.

SÉAMUS MACMURPHY

I heard mention of the poet Séamus MacMurphy – in fact there is a play in Gaelic about his betrayal – but my interest was renewed when I came across him again in Paterson's *Harvest Home*.

Séamus MacMurphy was a poet from Carnally in the parish of Creggan in the Fews in South Armagh. His ancestors had lived in an area near Caledon, where they were supplanted in 1172. They moved to the Fews where they were the earliest chieftains on record. The powerful clan O'Neill were extending south and eventually pushed them out of there too, so that by the early 1700s they were of a lowly status in society.

Séamus was a handsome and esteemed poet and is reputed to have attended a famous bardic gathering at Slieve Gullion in 1744. He became an outlaw and is said to have had two weaknesses: drink and women, and the story is told that he frequented a shebeen owned by Paddy Daker or 'Paddy of the Mountain' who peddled poitín. It was an awkward spot to get at for those not familiar with it, yet from there all the thoroughfares of the area could be observed and this made it suitable for the outlaws.

Paddy Daker held no interest for MacMurphy but his pretty daughter Mollie did, and she obviously held a torch for him. It was with some consternation that Mollie learnt from Art Fearon that MacMurphy had dalliances elsewhere. In spite of the fact that he was a close and trusted friend of Séamus MacMurphy, Fearon's jealousy had got the better of him, and he told her all this in the hope that she'd transfer her affections to him. He had very definite designs on her and was in fact set on marrying Mollie, so he was going to do the best he could to disenchant her of MacMurphy. Mollie was bitterly stung by Fearon's revelation and though she had no regard for the £50 that was on MacMurphy's head, her father had. Paddy Daker strove to persuade his daughter to betray Séamus and she eventually succumbed because she had been so hurt by news of his amorous exploits in other quarters.

The authorities, with the full knowledge of Séamus's good friend Art Fearon, were informed that he would be drinking at the shebeen on a particular Saturday night and that he would stay overnight to take Mollie on the pilgrimage to St Bline's (also called St Moninne) Well at Killeavey the following day. His 'good friend' Paddy Daker plotted to get MacMurphy blind drunk and have him transferred to Armagh Gaol and that's where Séamus found himself when he awoke from his drinking bout on Sunday morning – a far cry from the celebrations at the Holy Well.

Armagh Gaol in the eighteenth century stood somewhere at the bottom of Market Street. The former Market House, which is now the library, has been suggested but others would place it further down at the back of Scotch Street. In any case, it was a maze of underground apartments below the Sessions House. A flight of nine stairs led down to these, giving rise to the expression used in Armagh: 'They will go down the nine steps', meaning 'they'll come to a bad end'. The walls were 7ft thick and there was hardly any light in the cells. The executions took place on Gallows Hill – currently a hill out past St Malachy's Church on Lower Irish Street.

Although MacMurphy was gaoled in August, his trial and execution didn't take place until the following March. He was guilty of many crimes but that which he was actually hanged for was the stealing of a sheep. At that time you could be hanged for not just the theft of an animal but the theft of linen or of a firkin of butter.

At some time during those long months awaiting his trial, he wrote a lament. In a few lines from it we hear the loss experienced by a prisoner who has been used to living in harmony with nature:

> If I could only exist as a fern leaf in the
> Sunshine on Ardaghy Hill or on top of Fathom,
> or be a blackbird flying through Dunreavy Wood.

In those days, the procession to Gallows Hill from the gaol went up Market Street, over Castle Street and down Upper and Lower Irish Street. On this day there were comrades of MacMurphy in the crowd. The sheriff, officers of the law and the guard were all present. They say that Séamus MacMurphy forgave all those who had done him injury, especially his sweetheart Mollie. He was taken down after hanging for three days. Then his mother waked him in her barn in Carnally for two nights and he was buried among the poets in Creggan churchyard.

Mollie's father had attended the execution and returned to Armagh later to collect his 'blood money'. They say that though the 'powers that be' made use of him, they despised him for the part he played and they paid him the £50 in coppers (pennies), which they made him count before taking it away in a bag. This he had to carry the whole way home: a distance of 20 miles. He was obliged to travel by night and conceal himself by day in case he was robbed and apparently when he was within sight of home, he collapsed and died.

Mollie was left carrying the burden of guilt – one just as heavy. In spite of her lover's magnanimous gesture of forgiveness at the end, people didn't let her forget. At every opportunity they recited the poem Séamus had written in prison. She could bear the guilt and loss no longer and drowned herself.

Whether this is how things fell out or whether it is how the people thought they should have fallen out, we will never know for sure, but we can always wonder.

4

HUMOUR

I was delighted to come across the following two stories in the Journal of Keady & District Historical Society *(1993). They were written by Tommy O'Reilly. I have stayed reasonably close to the original text. Tommy has sadly passed on now but I hope these stories will keep the memory of him alive.*

THE NEW BROOM SWEEPS CLEAN

The events I'm going to tell you about took place in the first part of the twentieth century, when the price of alcoholic drink went through the ceiling. People protested loudly, wrote to the newspapers, put it on the agenda at public meetings and lobbied prospective MPs about it. It was all to no avail; so, contrary to their wishes and perhaps their better judgement, they had no other option than to make their own. All they needed was barley, sugar, a wee still, a bit of heather to flavour it and of course wood for fuel. To the consternation of everyone, the government declared this illegal and ordered the police to 'seek out, apprehend and apply the full rigour of the law to the makers and purveyors of this illicit liquor and destroy the apparatus for the making thereof.'

Now it happened that a new man took over Doonglass Barracks after the old sergeant retired, and like every new broom, he was determined to sweep clean. He set out to put the area in order, which in those days involved checking on dog licenses, lights on carts and bicycles, names on the shafts of carts and, above all, making sure that no one slipped into the pub thru' the back door after church on Sunday. At that time and indeed for a long time afterwards in the North of Ireland, public houses were closed on Sundays. Now as I indicated earlier, there was a harmless wee bit of distillin' going on out in the bog and people got worried that this meddlesome sergeant might just find out about it – so thorough was he in ferreting out the law breakers. So they decided to tip him the wink and put him on a false scent. They never thought it would have such consequences; they only wanted to take the wind out of his sails and lead a quiet life of harmless lawbreaking. It has to be said, though, that they hit on a very effective method of modifying the enforcement of the law.

When Mulrooney got information about a certain man who was making poitín and where he could be found, it was like a red rag to a bull and he delighted in the next round of the proceedings for he hoped to catch the culprit red-handed. Full of legal and moral zest, he rushed into the barracks to collect his right-hand man Riordan. Riordan was a gem to any new sergeant for he knew the area like the back of his hand and could advise on the character of every person in the locality.

'Come on Riordan, we're going on a mission.'

'What is it? Where to, sergeant?' replied the surprised Riordan. Missions weren't the order of the day in that part of the country – unless they were religious ones.

'Never mind,' replied Mulrooney. 'The walls have ears. I'll tell you when we're out the road. This will be an opportunity for you to see modern police methods at work.'

When they had gone a considerable distance outside the village Riordan ventured the question again.

'We are proceeding in the direction of Cornavick,' Mulrooney declared.

'Cornavick?' said Riordan, puzzled, and he started to go through in his head all the people who lived in that townland but he couldn't come up with any lawbreakers. 'Who would we be after there, sergeant?' he asked, bewildered.

'James McNamee!' said the sergeant proudly.

'McNamee?' gasped the sergeant.

I must explain at this juncture that James McNamee was a respected man, a good neighbour, a model of law and order and moreover a local District Councillor. There is no possible way anyone would suspect him of crossing the law.

'What would we want him for, sergeant?' asked Riordan, wondering, not for the first time since Mulrooney arrived, if the world as he knew it was falling apart.

'We will apprehend him for the possession of poitín, a still and the utensils for making it,' declared the sergeant confidently.

'Oh, I think you've got things wrong there,' said Riordan, but it was impressed upon him that it was not for him to question the authority of the sergeant nor to ask the reason why.

As they reached the brow of the hill, old Corny O'Hare's place came into view. McNamee had married old Corny's daughter and had come into the farm of land, which he worked to great advantage. They watched the house and sure enough there was a lot of coming and going there; there was even a pony and trap in the yard in front of the house.

'I wonder what all that commotion is about,' said Riordan.

'I've told you,' said Mulrooney. 'He's just made a run of poitín and those are the neighbours coming and going for the supplies.'

'Well, I can't believe it,' said Riordan at a loss. But there was no denying the activity around the house.

'Follow me!' ordered Mulrooney and he marched up the loanin' to Corny O'Hare's house like a general at the head of his army with the reluctant Riordan dragging his heels behind him. He didn't bother to knock on the door but lifted the latch imperiously and walked in. With a policeman's alacrity he took in the scene as he cast his eye round the room and it settled on a bath of fairly clear-looking liquid under the dresser. In a flash he had grabbed a mug from the dresser and taken a couple of scoops of the liquid which he put to his head and slugged, savouring the taste.

'Oh sergeant! What did you do that for?' cried Mrs McNamee in distress. 'All you'd to do was ask me for a drink. I would have given you whatever you wanted – even a wee whisky.'

'Sure, what harm?' said the sergeant.

'Och!' she said, very upset indeed. 'My father, old Corny, died last night and … we … och that's the water we washed the corpse in!'

The sergeant just reached the midden outside in time to be sick. Riordan had to borrow McNamee's pony and trap to take him to the local infirmary, where he was laid up with jaundice for the next month! The locals had meant to put a stop to his gallop but they hadn't meant to nearly kill him!

CAUGHT IN THE ACT

On the same subject of drink, there had been another member of the constabulary who had caused consternation to many a poitín maker. The senior policemen were, of course, from outside the locality to which they were posted. This, I suppose, guaranteed impartiality. In this case Matt Magee actually settled in Doonglass by marrying a local girl and when he retired they continued living in the area and he was well accepted by the locals.

One evening a small group of men, Matt included, were drinking together in the pub. Among them was Mickey Leonard, a well-known poitín distiller in his younger days, and the conversation came round to the policing of poitín makers in Matt's time as a policeman.

'Oh, I've a right few stories about that,' said Matt, 'but I'm ashamed to say I was as fond of the drink that time as any of them.'

The others were amazed at this because they'd never seen or heard of any signs of drink on Matt. He had played the part of the model policeman to perfection. He reminded them of a man called Ned Reilly, known by everyone as the 'Sparra' (Sparrow).

'Oh aye, a harmless oul' craythur but powerful fond ov the bottle, God rest him,' said Mickey Leonard, the former poitín maker.

Ned told them then about the night he himself was coming down by the graveyard when he spotted the 'boul' Matt' sitting on a low wall and looking exceedingly miserable. He questioned him as to what he was doing there in the middle of the night and told him he could have him up for loitering with intent. Ned told him that his tongue was sticking to the roof of his mouth, that he was dying of the drouth and all he wanted was a glass. Matt replied that the public houses had all closed hours ago, and, possibly with a little personal interest in the matter, asked him where he would expect to get drink at this hour.

'Sometimes Mosey Cowan [the local publican] laves the back windy open a wee bit at the bottom,' said Ned hopefully.

Matt Magee warned him sternly that that would be illegal entry and that he should go off home to his bed.

The policeman moved on round the corner then but he suspected that Ned might not take his advice, so he slipped into the doorway of a shop and kept an eye out to see what antics he might get up to. It wasn't long before he saw Ned making his way across the road and slithering over the back wall of Mosey Cowan's. Magee made his way up the main street to the front door of Cowan's pub and listened intently. There was definitely someone inside, so Ned must have succeeded in opening the window further and climbing in; he could hear him pussyfooting about in there. Magee was actually hoping that Ned would get his drink and depart without any ado when he heard a glass fall and smash. In the still of the night the sound echoed round the house.

Magee held his breath, hoping all hell wouldn't break loose, and then he heard the voice of Mosey's wife asking him if he'd heard the noise and had he remembered to put the cat out. When he told her he had and to go back to sleep she got more insistent, telling him he'd better go down and put her out again – that she must have come back in through the window and she'd have the bar wrecked. Mosey reluctantly said he would and when 'the Sparra' heard that he dived for cover under the bar and knocked over another glass in the process. Mosey came downstairs in his bare feet calling out 'Pussy! Pussy!'. Then, as he stepped on the broken glass, he yelled and uttered a string of oaths.

'The foots cut aff me, ye dirty oul' baste.' He bent down to feel for the glass and felt something else instead. It was Ned's hand and, desperately hoping that he would go along with the idea of the cat, Ned began to lick Mosey's hand and mew, putting up a great show, but Mosey didn't swallow it: 'Come outa there

ye varmint or I'll brain ye with one of them bottles!' and the frightened Ned began to yell, whether with fright or disappointed drouth is not clear.

At that stage Matt Magee thought he'd better intervene before half the street was woken up so he called for someone to open up the premises. He heard Mosey swearing at Ned and telling him to stay hidden and keep his mouth shut. When the door finally opened Matt saw in the light of a candle Mosey in his nightshirt and cut feet full of apologies for the fact that his cat had got in and knocked over some glasses.

'Is that so?' said Magee. 'You'll be telling me next that that cat can talk for I heard you tellin' her to keep her mouth shut an' get under the bar or ye'd strangle her.'

Mosey had to come clean and conceded that it was 'the Sparra' wandered in to steal a drink, but Magee said that everyone knew that poor Ned ('the Sparra') wouldn't steal anything from anybody and that the fact was that Mosey had drinkers on his premises after hours and, ostentatiously, he took out his little black book.

Mosey took fright and said he'd give Ned a bottle of 'good drink' and if the policeman could get him out the back door he didn't care what he did with him as long as he didn't put the publican in his little black book and ruin his reputation. Magee agreed and Mosey thanked him profusely. The policeman saw 'the Sparra' home and gave him a glass of the poitín and left him one for 'the cure' in the morning and then he went home and drank the rest of the bottle.

He dreamt that night that he was up in court with Mosey Cowan as the judge, and the jury was made up of District Inspectors, Head Constables and Sergeants. 'The Sparra' was the Prosecuting Counsel and he was yelling and pointing a porter bottle at him. The verdict was a life sentence. His own sergeant was getting the rope ready. He dropped – straight out of bed with the sheet round his neck and body.

The whole experience caused him such a fright that he 'took the pledge' – went off alcohol for the next twenty years until he left the police force.

Matt Magee left a few astonished companions in the bar that night.

It seems that when Tommy O'Reilly wrote these stories, many of the local people particularly enjoyed them because they remembered the actual characters involved, in spite of the fact that the names had been changed.

ARMAGH'S LITTLE VENICE

There was higher than average rainfall in early October 1958 in Armagh. However, when 2 inches fell on the 10th, some of the drainage pipes finally gave up the ghost, so to speak, and emptied into lower Scotch Street. The pipes that flowed from the demesne of the Protestant Primate of All Ireland were particularly overstretched. They were very old and finally gave way but fortunately the wall of the demesne stood firm. The ensuing rush of water flooded a place known as 'the bridge' at the bottom of Scotch Street. It also poured into Lower Barrack Street, popularly known as the Back Looter, and rather than allow extensive flooding of people's homes, the fire brigade took the initiative and pumped the excess water down into The Mall, the Georgian pride of Armagh.

It must have been dreadful for those who were affected but for everyone else in the town there was tremendous excitement because this inland town suddenly sprouted a lake. People flocked to The Mall from all over the town to see it. One brave man and his son launched a boat on the water to loud cheers from the spectators. They might as well have been witnessing the springing of a magic well with a wizard sailing his boat on it.

There was equal enthusiastic interest when the fire service went to lower Scotch Street and, with the aid of ladders, rescued people from their bedrooms into a boat – a scene rarely, if ever, witnessed in this part of Armagh. Of course, the Mill Row was flooded regularly but the poor people there had to deal with it themselves and it didn't get wide recognition, but in 1958 the situation all round The Mall area was generally regarded as a fabulous new spectator sport.

Gerry Hicks was described as an outstanding teacher in St Patrick's College in Armagh. He had an enormous influence on his students and was greatly respected by them. He was a man of many interests and was regarded as a loveable character as he cycled through the streets, frequently dismounting to chat to friends. He was a fine folk-singer and played the guitar. He sang on radio and recorded songs for the BBC folk archives and he composed humorous satirical songs. This is how he recorded the phenomenon of the flood.

The Armagh Rover

This is sung to the air of the 'Irish Rover' and reproduced here by kind permission of Gerry's daughter Eileen Hicks.

In the year '59* on a Saturday night
A storm came of thunder and rain,
And on the next day we all got a fright
As the floods burst from out the Demesne.
In Scotch Street as we stood to our oxters in the flood
Ben Hamilton did look the matter over,
He threw off his rubber coat saying, 'Boys we need a boat
And we'll call her the Armagh Rover.'

Then up from o'er the sea, came our chairman, Mr Gray
And him telling Paddy Byrne what to do.
He says, 'Run there in a hurry and we'll launch the bin lorry

With the Council men to act as a crew'.
Jimmy Reilly was the mate, so sober and sedate,
McGlone and McGinn followed gleefully,
And standing on a bin shouting orders through the din
Was the skipper, bould brave Paddy Joe McKee.

Then like Joxer and like Fluther they went down the back looter**
While the Scotch Street boys did give them a cheer.
Dr Woods gave them injections for to save them from infections
From the bould Orange blades of Jail Square.
So proudly did they go, till they came to Jenny's Row,
And the B men with terror did scream,
But they stuck to their guns, like true loyal sons,
Saying, 'Here comes a Fenian submarine!'

Oh this gallant ould craft, she was holed for and aft,
And the crew knew her sad fate was sealed.
Going by the City Hall, the green flag was over all,
Alfie Briggs shouts, 'Boys, never do yield!'
So out the Shambles Road the flying dustbin goes,
Mick Russell he gave her the once over.

Now the first of our ships is rusting in the dips.
That's the last of the Armagh Rover.

* '59 must have fitted better with the tune or sounded better than '58
** The back looter was what Little Barrack Street was called

Of course politics was not remotely involved in 'the flood'. This was a relatively peaceful time in local history and Gerry was simply interpreting the whole situation as heroic for the sake of parody.

If local farmers were expecting to lead their animals in two by two all were disappointed for the waters subsided within a day. By all accounts, though, there was great community cooperation with people voluntarily giving their labour to whatever needed to be done and the 'Little Venice' was once more returned to a green sward.

THE LEAPERS

The following little anecdote comes from Seán O'Boyle, who taught for many years at St Patrick's College in Armagh and was a well-known collector of folk songs. It was said that he added colour to Armagh in the 1940s and '50s. He recorded and presented Ulster folk songs for the BBC in the 1950s.

They tell a story in Armagh about a man from Culloville who went to America. One day he was walking over the Rockies and he was attacked by a bear. The two fought for a long time and at last the bear sank exhausted to the ground. And the man from Culloville put his foot on its head and shouted 'Culloville for Wrestlin!'

(*Ulster Folk Life*, vol. 3 (1957), p. 49)

Another tale of physical prowess was told by Michael J. Murphy in *At Slieve Gullion's Foot*. It concerns two men who went on to become showmen in New York, but it all started with a jumping contest in Dromintee, South Armagh.

The master, Patrick Hearty, judged the jumping competition in the school and Pat O'Hagan was deemed the winner with a jump of 16ft! It sparked off a fierce rivalry between himself and the boy who was his closest competition, Mike McAleavy. They practised so much that they left all the other boys standing – literally; they wished only to spectate because it would have been ridiculous to try to compete.

When they left school the spirit of rivalry continued and caused quite a stir in the rural area. They didn't need to actually see one another's feats since they would hear plenty about them anyway and no doubt money was bet on which man could outdo the other. Rumour was rife.

O'Hagan heard that McAleavy had jumped from one railway line to another – and that he had landed perfectly! McAleavy heard that O'Hagan had jumped into farm carts passing along the road. He had promptly shaken hands with the (no doubt alarmed) driver and jumped out again; and that he heard that McAleavy had jumped clean over the crossbar at a football match – presumably not during the match (what a way to score a point!).

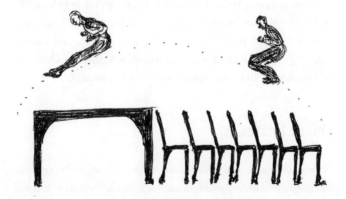

However, the excitement all stopped when McAleavy went off to work in Barrow-in-Furness.

In 1906, O'Hagan too went to join other Dromintee men in Barrow-in-Furness and when he met up with his old schoolmate they set up a gymnasium in a disused shed and got one of their friends from home to coach them. When a circus came to town, they entered the jumping competition; they had to jump over four horses lined up alongside one another! They both won prizes with O'Hagan coming first. This success opened up for them the possibility of making money from their skills. They went into training and styled themselves 'The McAleavy Marvels', performing in variety theatres in Great Britain, Belfast, Dublin and the theatre chain of Sir Alfred Butt. They proclaimed themselves 'The World's Champion Acrobatic Jumpers' and no one seems to have argued with that.

Off they headed then for New York to what was at that time the largest theatre in the world – the Hammerstein! Having done the rounds of other US theatres, they came back home for a short stay in 1911. Imagine the shock and surprise his old teacher Hearty and his companions got when O'Hagan suddenly flew through the air over their heads as they travelled along in a pony and trap.

Although both men have passed on now, people still remember some of their famous feats: jumping over a dining table and seven chairs from a springboard; with a stick across a barrel, jumping from the ground down one side of the stick, and down the other, and repeating the jump backwards; my favourite is 'with an alarm clock on a piano, jumping off a chair, releasing the alarm catch with the toe, thus setting the alarm off and landing' – all in one jump! What entertainment!

DRAIN JUMPER

Perhaps there was something in the water in County Armagh that encouraged the jumping gene because here is another instance of unusual ability. I came across it and the following story 'The Perils of Unrequited Love' in the Portadown Times. *They were written by 'The Chiel' who was both founder and owner of the paper and a local historian.*

In a different part of County Armagh we are told that the church at Mullabrack jumped across the road! Of course we're tempted to think of miracles but in this case it was nothing as interesting as divine intervention but rather road developments. The surrounding area is redolent with famous names. This Church of Ireland church was associated with the Culdees (*céile Dé*: companion of God), a semi-lay religious order back in the eighth century. Though in this case they think there may be seventh-century remains of the original structure lying beneath the much renovated present-day church.

The rector of this church from 1849 to 1859 was Lord John de la Poer Beresford, brother of the Primate Beresford. He was much liked by his parishioners and quite unconventional. He obviously enjoyed mixing with the locals because he was very fond of an old beggar woman who was over 100 years old. She had evidently been quite athletic in her day because she could still jump drains! When Beresford met her, he would give her a shilling for performing such a feat. He once invited her to jump over a straw rather than take on the task of a drain to prove herself. She was so offended that she tried to leap the nearest flax hole instead, but in her zeal she miscalculated the width and fell in. She might have drowned had Lord John not been there to pull her out.

He took her back home with him where she got dried out and was entertained by his wife, Lady John, who gave her fresh clothes to wear. This unexpectedly brought about the end of her jumping days. She told the disappointed Lord John that she wouldn't jump any more drains because she didn't 'think it seemly for her Ladyship's duds to be cuttin' such capers.'

The Perils of Unrequited Love

That same church at Mullabrack was the scene of a great passion – and not a religious one. Lord John had departed and the Revd Josiah Francis Flavell had taken his place. One of his congregation, Samuel Calliston, was besotted with a certain lady of the same congregation. She came from an old family of some standing in the area. It seems that a union was out of the question but it was not for want of trying on his part.

So frustrated was he in his failure to win her attentions that he took a pistol with him to church on Sunday, 17 January 1864 and, losing the run of himself during the sermon, he called out, 'There is no love in her heart for me, and I can live no longer!' Then he fired the pistol, causing consternation and pandemonium: women fled, some of them falling over one another as the billowing dresses of the time got stuck at the end of the pews.

Well, Calliston ended up in court and he spent part of his time there extolling the virtues of his idol. It also came out, much I'm sure to the lady's alarm, that he had spent entire nights in a tree near her house so that he might catch a glimpse of her in the morning! (Well that's what *he* said.) It also transpired that he was prone to taking on any other man who was foolish enough to express his admiration for her, with the result that he spent some time in Armagh Infirmary recovering from his injuries. It was obviously the age of Romanticism because people made pleas on his behalf, stressing the desperate situation of his unrequited love so that in the end he was sentenced to only two months.

The lady in question, though much admired, died single – which is just as well because Calliston would probably have murdered anyone who dared to marry her!

5

MURDER AND
RESURRECTION

LIVED ONCE, BURIED TWICE

This type of story is associated with many areas. I heard this story in brief from individuals in both Armagh and Portadown and each one insisted it was from their homeplace. I felt compelled to find the truth of the matter. Reports in the Armagh Gazette *(1924) revealed all for 'Lived Once, Buried Twice' and a story of long ago retold in the* Lurgan Mail *(April 1988) unfolded the story of Margery McCall. Redrock is an area about 4 miles outside Armagh City. The cemetery there is reported to contain a great deal of rock under the surface – with the result that graves weren't always dug down the statutory 6ft – which proved too much of a temptation for one would-be grave robber.*

There was a fairly young woman living in that area, a Mrs Lister. She was happily married with two children. Since she was a strong, young woman, everyone was shocked when she fell ill suddenly and, deteriorating rapidly, in a very short space of time passed away. There was great dismay at her dying 'before her time' and the neighbours greatly pitied her bereft husband and children. She was duly laid out and the coffin was placed on four chairs below the only window in the room. All the mourners who waked her commented, as they inevitably do, on how well she looked and how she looked in death just as she had in life – down to the redness of her lips.

Those who laid her out had tried to remove a lovely diamond ring from her finger but as it proved impossible it had to go with her to the grave. Amid great anguish she was finally buried in Redrock cemetery and her husband and children returned to a house that felt very empty indeed.

That evening, after their servant man had tended to the horses and cattle and eaten his supper, he slipped off under cover of darkness to the graveyard. He was carrying a kitchen knife, for, like everyone in the household, he knew about the diamond ring. Once in the graveyard he took a shovel and dug out the newly filled grave. His task was not so onerous on account of the grave being shallower than average because of the rocks underneath the surface.

When he prized open the coffin there lay the diamond ring, sparkling in the light of his lantern. He hoped he could haul it off the finger but after a strenuous effort he felt he had no more time to lose and he resorted to the knife. As the blade cut into the skin, the 'corpse' stirred and Mrs Lister opened her eyes to see someone leaning over her with a knife.

'Leave me alone! Leave me alone!' she spluttered, trying to understand what was happening and then she cried out loudly as she realised the danger she was in. The servant was alarmed. A hard-headed man, he had not expected to encounter anything as ghoulish as a corpse rising up to protest his crime. It was too much and he fled, never to be seen or heard of again.

The bewildered corpse was surrounded by darkness apart from the light of the servant man's lantern, which he had left behind in his haste. The poor woman could think of nothing else except to try to get out of the pit she was in and to reach some hopefully 'normal' world above, for it was hideous to find herself in what seemed to be a coffin. She lifted the flickering lantern and, by balancing herself shakily on the wooden side of the coffin, she was able to place it on the damp ground above, but clambering out of the pit was a different matter. A shroud is not the ideal garb for night-time climbing so when she reached the top of the pit she found herself dirty and shivering amid the tombstones in the graveyard.

At least she knew where she was then, so, covered in mud, she stumbled on bare feet towards the gate and down the road towards a glowing light that she figured was her own home. Shaking with cold and fright, hunger and weakness, and in a state of great confusion, she tapped weakly on the lit window of her house.

When her husband drew back the curtain he was greeted with the ghastly sight of a woman who bore a passing resemblance to the wife he had buried that afternoon. Greatly alarmed, he called the servant woman and when they opened the door his wife, filthy and with bleeding feet, collapsed into their arms. Between them they got her inside and upstairs into a bath of warm water to clean and warm her ice-cold body.

The doctor was summoned to attend to her. One can only imagine what his thoughts were when he was called out to someone he had pronounced dead. The patient lay ill in bed for some weeks afterwards but, to the surprise and delight of all who knew her, she emerged fully recovered at the end of it all.

Mrs Lister went on to bear several more children and she lived to a ripe old age. When she finally died, her headstone was inscribed 'Lived Once, Buried Twice'.

The facts of this account come from a descendant of the woman who worked in the Lister's house at the time. Indeed a sensational event like this would not be easily forgotten and the happy ending would ensure that it was passed on like a family heirloom.

What the servant man had attempted in that case was not so very unusual even in the present day. Grave-robbing, especially for jewellery, is widespread and has gone on for millennia. Of course it has been legitimized in cases where the plunderers are termed 'explorers' and the plunder 'museum artefacts'!

MARGERY McCALL

Another incident of this kind took place in Lurgan, County
Armagh around 1705. This time it involved a woman named
Margery McCall. There is historical evidence that in 1719 a John
McCall, thought to be her husband, was part of a deputation from
the Presbyterian congregation of Lurgan attending the synod. He is
also thought to have been part of an attachment to William III in
1689. It's believed that they lived in Church Place and Margery,
when she died, was buried in Shankill graveyard in Lurgan. Those
who laid out the body were unable to remove a valuable gold
wedding ring that she wore and she was sent to the grave with it.

They say that 'a villain of no fixed abode' overheard her friends
discussing the situation with the ring and, in the style of all good
grave robbers, he made his way to the graveyard at nightfall armed
with a shovel. He opened the grave and, failing to remove the
ring, he decided to amputate the woman's finger. With the first
cut of his knife, however, blood flowed (proving that the corpse
was living) and Margery 'rose and confronted him'. While the
latter is unlikely, I imagine any sign or stirring of life in a corpse
would be enough to scare off the most seasoned thief, and he was
no exception.

The story goes that the husband, in a mournful state, was
sitting by the fire with friends when a knock came to the door.

'If Margery were still alive, I would swear that was her knock,'
he said to his companions, and he left the room to open the door.

A burial and resurrection in the one day proved too much for
the poor man: at the sight of his wife in her shroud he fainted
clean away. Like the 'corpse' in the previous story, Margery McCall
survived for many years but in her case she bore only one more
child. When she finally died it's said that her headstone too bore the
inscription 'Lived Once, Buried Twice'. However, what is possibly
more interesting and certainly more convincing is that, according
to elderly Lurgan dwellers, the headstone was a replacement for an

older stone. They claimed that the earlier headstone recorded the date of both of her burials. What a shame it fell into disrepair.

If you think these women had an unfortunate experience, think again. They were extremely lucky that someone came to raid their grave. The *Portadown Times* reported a story that Thomas Best, a carpenter who had been employed by a contractor, had recounted to Archibald Annett. Annett was the sexton of the church in Tandragee and Best told him about an incident that still haunted him. In the course of his duties he had had to go into the St John vault. Oliver St John was given O'Hanlon land soon after O'Neill and O'Donnell fled to Rome in 1607. The O'Hanlon had supported O'Neill in the 1594-1603 rebellion.

Anyway, this carpenter opened up the vault and stood gaping at what was before him – the erect body of a woman. After the initial shock, the practical man took his rule and reached it out to touch the form. The shape disintegrated into dust. The conclusion? Well, there had been a lady visiting Tandragee a long time before and she had disappeared or died or … no one was quite clear about it. One can imagine that a visitor, interested in local history or researching their ancestors, might wish to enter a vault. If anyone has ever had difficulty opening a door they will know the panic that ensues and it wouldn't be easy to get help in a graveyard! The poor woman!

In case anyone should get the idea that the good citizens of County Armagh are in the habit of burying their living, it must be stressed that a story, similar to the 'coming back from the grave' ones, is told about a person in Wexford in the south of Ireland and likewise about someone in North Carolina and I have heard it told about a body in Glasnevin cemetery in Dublin. Perhaps every county has its living dead! To modern-day ears it may sound a little far-fetched but we must bear in mind that medical science is so much more advanced today with regard to detecting signs of life in people who, though they may appear dead, are simply in a coma.

The Green Lady's

Mary McVeigh from the Irish and Local Studies Library in Armagh was very helpful in furnishing me with the accounts of this story and transcripts of the court case in the Armagh Guardian *(March and April 1888). Seán Barden, from the County Museum, supplied me with the doubly tragic ending.*

As children, we often climbed the stone steps to Vicars' Hill. It's a secluded street of Georgian houses running alongside the Church of Ireland in Armagh. We went to look at 'The Green Lady's': this was one of the Georgian houses which was reputed to be, or have been, haunted. The scary thing about it was that it had a brick wall *inside* the window – about a foot from the window pane. I distinctly remember my fingers gripping the edge of the window sill (it was quite high so someone must have pushed me up) and on the inside window ledge I saw broken, blackened glass.

One midsummer more recently I went back there with a relative. We were on our way back to Belfast from a picnic with my cousin David Conlon, who invites us to his farm every year around midsummer. His farm lies between where my father was born on one side and where my grandfather and great-grandfather lived on the other. Midsummer's day falls around the feast of St John, which is celebrated in many countries. Like many of the Christian feast days, it was superimposed on one of the old Celtic festivals. Anyway, during the picnic by the river, I discovered that Feidhlm, who is interested in architecture, wasn't familiar with the Georgian buildings in Armagh so I gave him a brief tour on the return journey.

'And this,' I said, 'is Vicars' Hill where we used to come to look at "The Green Lady's". It has a brick wall inside the window.'

Well try as I might, I couldn't see any window with a brick wall visible thru' the window and yet I could have sworn I had seen it as a child. I was a bit disconcerted then and could see no one around who might corroborate my story. At last a man came into view and although I felt rather foolish, I approached him on the principle that if you don't ask you'll never find out.

'Excuse me,' I said, 'but could you tell me where "The Green Lady's" is?' I felt ever so slightly ridiculous.

'I live in it,' he said, which threw me completely. I was stuck for words – well it *is* a bit of a conversation stopper.

'Have you ever … did you ever …?' I muttered.

He very kindly took me out of my misery. 'Have I ever seen anything? No. But of course it was completely refurbished before I moved in. The only thing I have noticed,' he replied, 'is that my neighbour's dog will never come into the kitchen with him. The neighbour often calls round to the back of the house. He comes in to chat to me in the kitchen but the dog stands on the threshold and growls and the hair rises on the back of its neck. I'm a retired vet and I know that animals can sense things that humans can't.'

I was very glad I'd stopped him.

This happened around the year 2000 and I decided to try and find out the true story behind the house's fame. I already knew from a neighbour (Mrs O'Reilly who died at the age of 102) that the place should never have been called 'The Green Lady's'. It was a misnomer and that name actually belonged to the residence of another ghost in the town: to think that we'd wasted all those years speculating about whether she'd worn a green dress or if a priest had exorcised her and put her in a green bottle or just why was she green! But the name has stuck and to this day it's known by everyone in Armagh as 'The Green Lady's'.

The tale behind the house turned out to be very dark indeed.

In 1888, a woman called Nina Prior lived in that house. She was the widow of Colonel Prior, who had been commander of the military district of Armagh. She lived there with her daughters Adele (21), Bellina (19), and her son Harvey (14) who attended the Royal School – a famous school in Armagh founded in 1608. The family were very well connected and, by all accounts, well liked by different classes of people in the town.

The story also involves a family by the name of Slavin, who lived below Vicars' Hill in Callan Street. A little girl in that family, Kate, used to do messages for the Priors. She was nine years old and would knock on their door to see if they wanted her to get anything for them. When she returned with whatever they'd asked her for, she'd be given a few sweets.

On Tuesday 27 March, Nina Prior left the house between 1.30 and 2 p.m. and Kate Slavin called at the door around 3 p.m. She had with her her little sister, Ann, who was three years nine months old at the time. Bellina answered the door. It was said that Bellina was fond of the local children and would often spend her pocket money on sweets for them. She was described as a petite and very attractive girl. She was quite taken with Ann and told Kate that they didn't need any messages that day but suggested she leave her little sister with them till 4 p.m.

Kate went off and Bellina carried the little girl upstairs to where Adele was playing the piano. They both made much of the little one and Adele gave her a barley sugar sweet and then Bellina took her downstairs to the kitchen. About a half an hour later Bellina came back upstairs to Adele 'looking red eyed and with a mad look' on her face.

'Where's the little girl?' Adele asked.

'I've killed her,' Bellina replied.

Adele went downstairs with her and saw a truly horrific sight. A boiler was standing above a cooking range in the kitchen; it was used for boiling up water for the household and now, from the top of the boiler, two little feet protruded. Adele sent for her mother and she herself got the little girl out, hoping to save her, and she placed her on the inner ledge of the window which she fitted exactly – her body being 37 inches long – but the child was already dead.

Nina went to fetch Chancellor Benjamin Wade and sent her son Harvey for Dr Gray. Chancellor Wade asked Bellina if she knew what she had done. They say that she didn't answer for a long time but just gave a maniacal smile before saying, 'I've killed her. Everyone is unkind to me. Mother I have paid you off and I'm glad of it.'

He then asked her if she understood the consequences of what she had done and she replied, 'I will be hanged, I suppose, and I will be glad of it.' And she smiled again. Chancellor Wade sent for the constabulary and District Inspector Bailey arrived. Adele told them how Bellina's behaviour had been strange during the last six weeks or so. She described how Bellina had raised a hatchet to them the previous Thursday. However, they took it as a joke since they were accustomed to Bellina's fooling around. When she tapped Adele on the head with it the latter took it away from her.

It turned out that Kate Slavin had returned for her sister that afternoon and Bellina had rapped the window and told her to leave her with them until 6 p.m., saying that she was 'a pretty little thing'. When word of what had happened spread that evening a crowd gathered in the street outside the house, discussing the terrible turn events had taken.

As soon as the police had finished questioning her, Bellina was taken off to prison. The child's body was kept where it was overnight under police guard and the inquest took place next morning. Part of the inquest was held in the house, where they decided to take the evidence of the very distressed Adele.

The coroner and the jury then returned to the Tontine where Joseph Slavin, the child's father, was questioned. Slavin was a whitewasher by trade and was described as a decent, hard-working man. Then Drs Gray and Palmer, having examined little Ann, reported that she was a healthy, well-developed, well-nourished child and that her death was by drowning. The verdict of the jury was death by manslaughter against Miss Bellina Prior.

The decision to hold the court case on Saturday morning was unusual. The matter was kept very quiet with the result that the crowds of interested Armagh residents were not in attendance. This would have been to accommodate this very well connected family at such a trying time for them. While the matter was tragic for the Slavins, they were a poor family of no account. Such is the way of the world.

Constable McGee ushered Bellina in. She was 'closely veiled'. The matron of the gaol sat on her right and Sergeant Maxwell on her left. Nina Prior, when questioned, spoke of her daughter having fainting fits and a headache about a month before the event. She also mentioned that her daughter had had a severe fainting fit in London about a year before. Her mother admitted that she had wanted Bellina to go on the stage and that Bellina had been very anxious and worried about it. She also recounted how Bellina had gone down to the kitchen one night to fetch some water and had seen a man's face at the window, making her quite paralysed with fear.

In the course of the various pieces of evidence that followed, it transpired that there was a chair and a partially covered can beside what was described as an open boiler. The police measurements put little Ann at 37 inches and one of the cans at 14 inches and the top of the boiler from the can at 22½ inches. It seems there had been 12 inches of cold water in the boiler. Dr Gray vouched that he and Dr Palmer had found no sign of violence on the child's body, that they had found the barley sugar mixed with other food in her stomach, and had pronounced a case of death by drowning. He had made a number of calculations to ascertain if this drowning could have happened accidentally and he expressed the opinion that it was possible.

Dr Palmer also claimed that Bellina had very possibly been in a state of shock, unable to help the child because of this and liable to falsely accuse herself of having drowned the little one. Although the solicitor for the accused asked for her to be charged with manslaughter since there appeared to be no malice aforethought, the judge, Captain Preston, said he would have to 'return the accused for trial on the capital charge'. There was a dead silence in the courtroom, which was finally broken by Bellina's sobbing. The family were overcome with pity and were given permission to go to her, whereupon her mother threw her arms around the girl and showered her with affection. When she calmed down a little, Bellina, in a small voice, apologised to her mother for the trouble she had caused her. Afterwards Constable McGee and the matron accompanied her in a close carriage to the County Gaol. Those present in the court had great sympathy for the Prior family and indeed were appalled by the whole affair.

Apparently, during her brief stay in prison, Bellina had tried to cut her throat with glass, though she made little of it, saying it was nothing but a scratch. After five minutes the jury found her to be insane at the time of the murder and the judge ordered that she be kept in custody as a criminal lunatic. It is said that the family moved south after a time and Bellina was transferred to a mental institution there.

It was suggested that they may have moved to England after that but it seems proof has been found that Bellina was released from hospital and went back home to live with her mother. They had various addresses in Dublin, the last of which was in Rathmines, where the mother is said to have bought poison and given it first to her daughter and then taken it herself because their life was so intolerable. Whether it was to do with Bellina's state of mind or very possibly because their history followed them everywhere they went, we don't know.

Their deaths were reported in the *Irish Times*. Further information came to light in letters held in Armagh Museum. There it was indicated that Nina Prior was not regarded as being the best of mothers. And so ends the story of 'The Green Lady's'.

THE TOULERTON MURDER

There was a very full account of this story and the court case in the
Portadown Times *(1936).*

In 1788 John McNeely, an elderly farmer, had the rental of a
farm on land that lay on the old road from Portadown to Lurgan.
McNeely's daughter was married to James Toulerton and, on
account of the guaranteed low rent, a nominal fee, the farm was
coveted by James' family. One would have thought there should
be no envy of the McNeely's farm since old John was going to
leave it to his grandson, of whom he was very fond. However,
the child was still an infant at the time so the Toulertons might
have a long wait. Moreover, McNeely was a widower and in
good health so there was always the danger that he might up and
marry again and the Toulertons would never get their hands on
the land.

These Toulertons were a 'bad lot', indeed they brought such
fear and terror into the hearts of the district that one would
nearly have called them evil. James Toulerton's brother, John,
was described as being of 'weakish intellect', implying that he
was malleable – he did, however, appear to take on with gusto
whatever malevolent role he was assigned. This made him a very
convenient pawn for his father, old Saunders Toulerton, who,
it seems, was the prime mover in the horror I will now unfold.

One Friday night in 1788, when John McNeely was sleeping
in his bed with his young grandson fast asleep beside him,
the Toulertons entered the house and, after removing the boy
from the bed, John hit McNeely a blow with a hatchet. James and
his father, old Saunders Toulerton, then dragged the body from
the bed and bled it over a crock.

It so happened that half a mile from there, lying nearer to
Portadown, was the dwelling of Robert Wilson. He had gone to
Lurgan market that day and, since it was now late and he hadn't

returned, his wife was very anxious and decided to go out in search of him. She took with her a lad of eighteen, McCullion, who was apprenticed to her husband. Now Robert Wilson was very friendly with John NcNeely so when she got as far as McNeely's she thought she'd make enquiries there. Of course she was reluctant to knock them up at that hour of the night so she and the young lad went round the back of the house to see if there was any sign of life or if a light was still lit.

A little light was shining out of one window and when she peered in she saw that an old waistcoat hung inside to serve as a curtain but a light was filtering through a rent in the waistcoat. As she peered in through the tear in the waistcoat she was aghast! The Toulertons were in the process of bleeding the dead body of McNeely! Horrified, Mrs Wilson and the McCullion lad fled and in the ensuing days they remained dumbstruck. It seems that fear of these Toulertons was enough to silence all the neighbours, even about their heinous crimes. In fact no one ever dared enter their house.

Meanwhile the perpetrators of the crime had removed the corpse to a loft of wickerwork known as a 'skey'. Nevertheless, by the time three days had passed, enquiries were being made and rumours were afoot. Anyone who enquired was told that McNeely had gone to County Antrim and would be back in a few days.

The Toulertons thought it wise to remove the body to a deep bog drain in an uncultivated morass that divided the townlands of Ballyhannon and Bocombra. Indeed this might have guaranteed that their crime would never have been discovered were it not for a magistrate, Mr Workman of Magha. He had resolved to improve the safety in the area and to bring some ease to a very troubled neighbourhood – troubled, that is, by the activities of the Toulertons and their friends. He began to make enquiries and set about ferreting out the truth about John McNeely's whereabouts. This rattled the Toulertons somewhat. They thought it best to send John away in case, with his slow-mindedness, he let the cat out of the bag. Of course this caused further alarm, because people wondered if they had done away with John as well, for old Toulerton had previously been suspected of killing his own wife. (They were obviously charming customers!) So the old man and James dug up McNeely's body, put it in a sack and tied it up. At dead of night they took the sack on a cart past the Bann River to Knockbridge and headed for the Newry Canal.

At this juncture the story was witnessed and elaborated on by a man called Hugh Dempsey. It seems a valuable mare was expected to foal and two men were employed to watch it at night. On the night in question, between twelve and one o'clock, one of these men, Dempsey, went to buy whiskey in Knockbridge. He heard the cart coming down the cross-lane from Lurgan Road – a strange enough thing to hear in this spot so late at night.

Perhaps he was emboldened by the whiskey or perhaps he hadn't yet drunk any and was sober enough to have his wits about him, but he quickly hid and took in the scene that confronted him. James was leading the horse and the father was on the cart with a sack full of something. Curious, Dempsey followed them to Knockbridge, saw them stop and take stones from the battlements and bring them up a trackway in the direction of Newry Canal.

Dempsey was not the only witness that the ever-thorough magistrate Mr Workman managed to locate. A young man, McConville, also observed this event at close quarters, where the road passes old Chapel Hill. When he caught sight of the 'removal', both the Toulertons were at the horse's head. The cart passed so close to him that when he put his hand on the sack he felt what seemed to be feet. This time, unlike when Dempsey observed them, the murderers were aware of his presence as he passed.

Next day McConville saw old Saunders Toulerton approach his house and just had time to grab a pistol which he held at the ready up the wide sleeve of his greatcoat, for he knew that Toulerton wasn't prone to paying social visits. He decided that they must have recognised him the night before when they were engaged in whatever their most recent foul deed was. Toulerton said to him, 'We are in your power.'

'In my power?' said McConville, feigning astonishment. 'How can that be?'

'You met us on the road last night.'

McConville knew better than to acknowledge that. He understood that he might not live to tell the tale. So he proceeded to deny ever having stepped outside the house on the previous night and old Toulerton, apparently appeased, went away.

Well, the body was found some time later by a boatman in the Newry Canal. The sack had the stones from the battlements in it to ensure that the body would sink. With the help of Edward Montgomery, the boatman managed to get the body out. Montgomery had known McNeely well and was able to identify him. This was the first breakthrough for Workman because the Toulertons' assertion that McNeely was in County Antrim was proved false. They were arrested but the evidence was so lacking that the Toulertons got bail until their bailers feared they might abscond and they locked them up again.

When it came to the next assizes, Workman had Dempsey and Mrs Wilson and the young McCullion as witnesses. However, when McCullion was asked his opinion of Mrs Wilson he said that he had always thought well of her until he discovered that she intended to discount everything he said that day. And true enough, when she gave her evidence, she denied ever leaving her own house on the night in question! Workman must have got wind of what she was going to say because he had another person at the ready who had witnessed Wilson and McCullion on the road to McNeely's. Workman's hard work paid off and when the pair were pronounced guilty old Toulerton is reputed to have called out 'Mercy!' but the judge said, 'Mercy you did not show and mercy you cannot expect'.

The execution was ordered on the hill of Clanroll, near the scene of the crime. It was separated from McNeely's house by a ravine. It's reputed that 1,000 people witnessed it. From the execution spot, a lane led down to the great Lurgan Road, where stood a huge fragment of rock known as the Blue Stone (because of its colour) – hence the name of the surrounding area. Workman ordered the bodies to be put in a deep pit underneath the rock and the rock was rolled into the hole on top of them. Incredible though it may seem, a party of men from Moira, friends or relatives of the Toulertons, came during the night, raised the stone and propped it up. They then attempted to get at the smashed coffins and retrieve the bodies, presumably to bury them elsewhere.

On hearing of this, Workman, with a force of men, arrived to raise and burn the bodies on the road and sweep the ashes into the pit and roll the stone back once again. Everything was filled in and secured and it was hoped that no bodies would surface again. However, there's room for doubt, because it wasn't until this point that McConville revealed his secret.

He had been so deeply shaken by the event that he had no intention of talking about it to anyone. He was courting the daughter of John O'Hara of Bocombra, who later became his wife. O'Hara incidentally lived near the place where McConville had met the cart on that ill-fated night. One night the rain was so heavy McConville couldn't go back home and so slept, along with the girl, in the upper room or loft. He awoke to see a darkness at the window and a low voice said, 'McConville, McConville, I was murdered innocent.'

McConville was terrified, so much so that he crept behind the young O'Hara girl, who neither saw nor heard anything. The event serves to show how deeply affected the young man's mind was and it wasn't till the Toulertons were buried for the second time that he revealed his secret. It would seem that bodies buried round Armagh were in the habit of resurrecting themselves with indecent frequency!

6

THE
'GOOD FOLK'

THE FAIRY MAN

George Paterson, born in 1888, was a remarkable man. He was a country boy from the townland of Aghory, County Armagh and from his early days he showed an interest in just about everything he came across. Since his family weren't in a position to educate their eight children, he became an apprentice in Davison Brothers' grocery store in the town of Portadown, 5 miles to the north of his home. He later worked for Couser's in Armagh City and had the habit of making notes on interesting things he saw and heard about, so from an early age his passion for recording local history and folklore was evident. From his humble beginnings he became a member of many organisations, sat on numerous councils, committees and boards and contributed to a great number of very reputable journals. In 1941 he was elected to membership of the Royal Irish Academy. In 1945 Queen's University Belfast awarded him an MA and in 1954 he received an OBE. He is probably best known in County Armagh as the curator of Armagh Museum.

He spent a great deal of time locating and finding out about ancient monuments, particularly in South Armagh, and

everywhere he went he collected folklore. South Armagh was
particularly rich in fairy lore and it seems he had great skill in
the speed and accuracy with which he recorded local speech.
He travelled by motorbike and one sunny day he left his bike by
the side of a quiet country road and, stepping into a nearby field,
he stretched himself out in the long grass beyond the hedge to
study his map. Along the way came two forty-year-old locals to
whom he had spoken earlier. They saw his bike and, assuming
that he had climbed the nearby hill, proceeded to discuss him.
Paterson abandoned his map reading and started to write down
their conversation. After his death the record of the conversation
was found among his papers and published at the end of a book,
Harvest Home, which contained part of his extensive research.
I have included the original transcript here, along with a few
annotations to add clarity:

'That's his bike (long pause). Bedam an' it's a comfortable saddle
he hez. I wonder what he wants with the oul' stone [the ancient
remains]? D'ye think did he hear of the gold? I believe he's the very
fella wee John's Hughie saw on the mountain above steppin' the
stone he wus – north, east, south and west. An' he hed a thing on
three legs [a camera on a tripod] an' wus bludy hard till plaze as till
how it wud stan'.'

'Ay, an' the wee ones wur hooking it home from school at the
time. An' he hed apples an' cakes an' they'd a sup of tay together.
A tin cup he hed, an' filled their heads with fancies he did. "What
does the oul' people be sayin'?" says he' (laughter).

'An' he hed wee slices of bread wi' greens inside. The childer
said they wur bludy good, an' he axed [asked] them their history.
Herself [his wife] wondered what hed happened till them at all, at
all. Sure if they see him the day, they'll not lave him till night. He's
a bit of a chile heself I'm thinkin'.'

'What is he anyhow? Sure it's a quare taste he has. Says he likes
oul' things. I wonder how he'd like my oul' duds. Sure it's swop

him I wud. But mind ye he's pleasant spoken. It's a pity he hasn't more sense than till be botherin' with oul' stones an' the like.'

'An' did ye hear him about the bludy cashel! A relig, he says, mains a burial place of sorts. Bedam an' it bates the bludy ban', how he knowed that. Sure it wus only the oul' people iver knowed that dead childer wur iver buried there.'

'He must hev little till do or he'd niver hev time till be galli-vantin' the country over! On top of Carrick he wus an' sat in Patrick's Chair. That's more than I've iver done, mind ye, an' me within a mile of it all me life. It's up I'll go on Bilberry Sunday for it's shamed I'd be to hev him axe me again. But sure if he hed till work for a living it's little huntin' of oul' stones an' forths he'd do. An' Patrick's long dead anyhow.'

'What does he be wantin' here unless he heared about the bludy goold? Has he anything till do wi' lan' do ye think?'

'Ye main one of them misureing fellas?'

'That's what a do.'

'Not he! Sure they only misure for the lan'lord or the govermint. Divil a hate the likes of them care about oul' stones. Nobody iver heared tell of one of them ones axin' after traditions!'

'If he'd said oul' yarns right away we'd hev knowed what he wanted. He an his bludy what-do-ye-call-thems. It's well you're the scholar for troth an' I'd niver have tumbled. Ah well! He's aisy plazed anyhow. Di ye think is he simple-like?'

'Och, the divil a simple. I've heared of people who'd them tastes afore – but I disremember the word.'

'Ah well! We must be gittin' along. I wish I hed he's way of travelling. Did ye see how he speeled the hill? But we may go on or it's back he'll be comin' an' wonderin' what we want with his bludy machine.'

'I'd like till sound the horn.'

'Is it daft ye are, an' the bludy man on the hill above ye?'

'Sure an' he'll niver know but it's a car on the broad road beyant.'

'Bad scran till ye, man; will ye lave that bludy machine alone?'

'To be sure an' I will. But I can't help thinkin' it's a pity it takes him that way. Di ye think is he a writer of books? Did ye see how fast he cud work his pencil? He'd hev the things written as fast as ye'd tell him. Mebbe you an' I'll be in print one day.'

'Who wants till be in a bludy book? Sure an' bedam an I'd rather hev me photer tuk any day. Am sure that's a thing for takin' likenesses he hed clipped on he's shoulder in thon wee bag.'

'Well he wus good crack anyhow – why didn't ye axe him?'

'A wonder what he does. Di ye know I'd lek right well till see him again. I wonder what he does now?'

'Takes an interest in oul' things didn't he tell ye!'

'Did ye see he's bludy coat? A'm thinkin' it's oul'. But then I'm sure he's dacent in under. Them fellas don't care about a tear or two. A wonder is he simple? He'd take down anything ye'd tell him. Di ye mind how he covered the paper?'

'Simple he's not. But it's a pity all the same that he hasn't a likin' for sensible things. Ah well! He'll git on all right with the oul' people. An' won't they be glad till git someone till listen till their oul' cracks! It's well we thought of Kelly. Sure it's Kelly an' he will sort like a house on fire.'

'Ay, they're both simple-like. Sure an' bedam and there's divil the differs atween them. Kelly believes in the wee people an' so does he or he'd niver be runnin' this oul' loanin' lookin' for what di-ye-call-thems.'

'Traditions.'

'Come home ye bludy fool – mebbe he's a fairy heself.'

(T.G.F. Paterson, *Harvest Home* (Dundalk: Dundalgan Press, 1975), pp. 212-14)

Fairy Lore

I have made ample use of Paterson's Country Cracks *in the following sections of fairies.*

George Paterson, as a keen folklorist, collected so many anecdotes about fairies that I defy anyone to read his *County Cracks* and not begin to wonder if maybe it were just possible that in the past fairies did exist. However, when you hear that they arrived in, and eventually left, Ireland in 'eggshell steamers' you stop wondering! It is said they left after the arrival of St Patrick with his new religion of Christianity, and that they didn't much care for this religion or for those who preached it. There were, reputedly, people who were fond of fairies and others who had some kind of affinity with them.

Very few of the inhabitants in South Armagh, where Paterson collected most of his folklore, believed that fairies were still around in the 1920s and '30s. In fact, a number of them recounted how the fairy folk had told a few chosen people that they were going to Wales to help some of their race who were at war there. When asked if they would return they said that that depended on the outcome of the war and that these friends would be able to find out what had happened by looking in the well water: if it was clear then the fairies would have won the war in Wales but if it was the colour of blood, then they would never be seen again. Another friend was told that if the berries came before the flowers on a certain old tree on his land, the fairy folk would never be seen again. It was said that they all gathered at Darby's Bridge before they left the country. Well the berries came before the flowers that year.

Perhaps that's why most of Paterson's accounts come from those who say, 'I never saw them myself but my father often saw them,' or, 'There were a lot of them about in my grandfather's time.' What is interesting is that there were certain places that were particularly associated with them and quite often the people who lived on those farms were sympathetic to them. What is absolutely clear is that people in general were afraid of them and went out of their way not to offend them and they were respectfully referred to as 'the good folk' or 'the gentry' while others believed them to be 'fallen angels'.

There were those, as well, who claimed they were left over from when the Tuatha Dé Danaan (a race of small people capable of magic who were followers of the goddess Dana) had lived in Ireland. That was before the Celts came.

FAIRY SIGHTINGS BY PEOPLE ALIVE TODAY

I collected these accounts from people in County Armagh in the autumn of 2013.

A man in his seventies from Portadown, a retired schoolteacher, told me that he saw a fairy once when he was a child. His grandfather was buried in Drumcree churchyard in the 1940s. The area was all countryside at the time with none of the present-day building developments. He was walking with his grandmother, who was wheeling a pram up the slope of the hill, and he saw a very small figure running up by the hedge alongside them. It seemed to dodge in and out of the hedge, peering out at them, and then it ran on. He had the impression that it looked rather like the traditional images of fairies but after seventy years he couldn't remember the details because he was only six or seven when he saw it.

'The strange thing is,' he said, 'that I never told anyone – which is unnatural for a child who would have been excited and would want to tell everyone. The normal thing would have been to blurt it out to my grandmother or rush to tell my parents when we got home. But I never told a soul until comparatively recently. Now it doesn't matter to me what people think. And I still have the memory clearly in my head.'

A woman whom I've known for years told me of something she'd seen as a child. This is her account:

There was a group of us together; it was someone's birthday and we were having a party. I suppose our mothers thought it would be a good idea for us all to go out to the Navan Fort (Emain Macha). It's so pleasant and peaceful out there and we were able to run around and let them get a chance to sit and chat. Well, it was a nice sunny day and they told us to go off and play so we went towards the mound and were trying to run up it.

Some of the children were in front and others at various stages behind. I was at the front with several others and as we came to the top there was a man of about 3ft coming towards us with a black dog. I can remember him really clearly to this day because he was so unusual looking: he was a grown man in the sense that he was mature – even though he was only 3ft tall – and he was wearing a suit. His skin was black, which was a very odd thing in those days. We would never have seen a black person – there just weren't any in Armagh at the time. I've often tried to think how he could have been there – if he could have been visiting any of the families around, but I couldn't find an explanation for it.

The dog was up to his shoulders he was so small, and it was a bit like a labrador. I remember the man had an open, friendly kind of face and a hairline that was quite far back – not a receding hairline but more like a high forehead. Well the Navan was supposed to be a magical place where you might see fairies or whatever so that's what we thought he was. Mind you, he didn't fit with what we thought a fairy would be: like you'd think a fairy would have gossamer wings and be sitting on a toadstool! But we had no other name for him so we ran back screaming to our parents that we'd seen a fairy. The ones behind didn't see him because they took fright when they heard us scream and ran too.

All our mothers said was that we shouldn't have run away because that meant we'd never see a fairy again. We discussed it a few times afterwards but later, as adults, we'd drifted apart so we never really consulted one another again to verify it, but I've often sought an explanation for it and found none.

Since I know that woman and the place, I understand what an unusual experience it was and I've wracked my brains too as to how or why the man might have been there. All I could come up with is that he might have been part of a travelling circus. But then, children would usually know if there was a circus in town. It's a puzzle.

FAIRY HELPERS

The information about the road at the end of this piece is from 'The Chiel', the Portadown Times.

Sometimes – though not often – the fairy folk befriended people. There was a woman one time who had lost a number of children and because of that she was very anxious about her new baby. She had it in a cot in the corner of the room and she was sitting there worrying about whether it would survive or not. In walked a very small woman; they greeted one another and began to chat. People didn't lock their doors in those days and they always made strangers welcome, usually giving them a drink of milk or tea. If it was a person who travelled the road and especially if they were known to them from other years or seasons they might give them food or even let them stay the night.

This little woman suddenly commented on the poor state of health of the child: 'That chile's not thrivin'. Take ye my advice an' move the cradle till the other corner or ye'll lose it altogither.' Then she walked out of the house, leaving the owner even more concerned about the child. She decided to do as the 'wee woman' advised her. She moved the cradle in spite of the disapproval of her husband since, in doing so, she had ousted him from his favourite seat in the room. The child began to flourish and grew up fit and strong and she didn't lose it after all. The woman who told this story said that it had come down to her from her mother and grandmother.

The fairy folk gave wealth to a favoured person on condition that they never tell anyone where it came from. Of course the person often broke the promise and they subsequently lost all their wealth. However, the fairy folk's reputation was more one of mischief and they seemed to like nothing better than to tease and torment people. They played childish games like tag around the plough in the fields and would pull the coat tails of men or women and then hide from them. They were generally pleased but quick to take umbrage and one was never quite sure what would displease them. An instance of their pleasure was when they were playing music one night on Coney Island in Lough Neagh.

Coney Island, it seems, was the poitín makers' paradise because there were no houses on it and so there was less chance of the men getting caught at their illegal activity. Two men who were working at their still, heard the music of the fairy flutes and bagpipes and then the players appeared to them. Each party, however, kept their distance with mutual respect, but the men, when they were going home, made sure to leave a little whiskey for the 'wee folk'. When they came back the next day the whiskey was gone so they continued to leave a drop every time they had finished their work. They figured it brought them luck since they were never caught by the constabulary and the whiskey was always gone when they went back. Someone enjoyed it anyway – whether it was the fairy folk or the constabulary themselves or some other knowledgeable party. And it's just possible that the men tested the poitín, the strength of which is well known to make people see and hear things that aren't always there!

Incidentally, Coney Island was the end of an ancient road which St Patrick ordered to be built so that materials could be transported to Armagh for the building of his cathedral there. Apparently there are remnants of this road still to be seen. It is said too that he went to Coney Island for prayer and meditation – they don't mention the poitín!

Forts and Lone Bushes

One way that was known to court the dangerous displeasure of fairies was to tamper with their forts. These, like the fairy bush, the hawthorn, were regarded as sacred and must not be touched. The owner of land near the village of Meigh decided to break up what was regarded as a fairy fort there, but he fell ill and died before he finished. The informant in that case claimed to have seen many fairies in that place and claimed they were still all around. Perhaps they didn't all go to Wales!

A man who tampered with what was thought to be a 'fairy ring' at the Navan Fort (Emain Macha) had a fate worse than Finn McCool (who dived into the Slieve Gullion lake and his hair turned grey); this man was left bald on one side of his head!

The Navan Fort featured again when word got about one time that there was treasure buried there. A group of young men made their way to the spot armed with shovels. However, as they got near the place, their courage began to fail them but each man was loath to be the first to cry off and so they began to dig.

In Ballyheridan an extremely wealthy man, who had a dozen racehorses in England, broke up a local fairy fort and subsequently lost all his money. (I don't suppose he ever gambled?) And another man in the same townland burnt his fairy thorn 'An' he wasted right away an' he a man of thirty four acres'. I'm not sure if it was the land or the man that wasted away – perhaps both.

One time Rathtrillick Fort near Middletown had flax sown in it. People said that the crop wouldn't thrive but it did – that is until the night before it was to be pulled, when it simply disappeared. Similarly corn was sown at what was known as the *Relig* (burial place) at Cashel and though people feared for the man who had sown it nothing at all happened to him and the crop was one of the finest ever seen. The morning they came to cut it, it had completely disappeared and there wasn't even stubble there to indicate that someone else had cut it. It was never sown again, such was the fright it gave everyone. Near Clay Lake was a fort that was set with potatoes one year and the owner thought nothing of breaking up the ground but they lost all their cattle that year and never tried to cultivate it again.

THE FAIRY FOOD

A yarn is told about a local man in Granemore who fell in with a fairy band of merrymakers but for some reason he suspected that they were fairy folk. Once he felt things weren't quite right he tried to leave the party but they pressed him to dance and drink their whiskey. He refused their whiskey though the more he danced the thirstier he got but managed to persevere in his refusal of the drink. It was well known that if you ate their food or drank their drink you were theirs forever.

A man was walking home late one night when he met a very small man and woman who asked him where the chapel in Clady was. When he told them they asked him to accompany them for a while – to 'lave us a bit of the road'. As they walked along the little man asked if he would like to share supper with them but our man became suspicious at this and said he had eaten before he came out. They arrived then at a place where there was a fire going with bread cooked on a kind of pan on top of it. The little man took the bread and broke it in two, giving him half and a half-crown as well – no mean amount in those days. Instead of trying a piece of the bread, he put it in his pocket along with the half-crown and walked on as fast as he could until he got to the next house. Then he put his hand in his pocket and there was nothing there but a stone. As he ran the rest of the way home he swore that, for love or money, he would never go out late again.

A couple of men from Corran had a similar fate when they were coming home from a wake. When they reached the local fairy fort they were asked to join in the merriment, and dance they did to their heart's content. They refused all offers of food and drink, but, so as not to offend the fairies, they accepted money from them. Next morning, lo and behold, the money had turned to stones.

These accounts are reminiscent of Christina Rossetti's long poem *Goblin Market*.

THE CHANGELING

Someone who didn't get off quite so lightly was Nancy of the Man's Coat. It seems that everyone knew that Nancy had been taken by the fairy folk to Killeen Fort and that she had spent three whole days with them. Neither food nor drink had passed her lips in the three days but needless to say she was never the same again. They say she was a familiar sight around Newry, wearing a man's coat with a needle and darning wool inside it – a way of warding off the fairies – and she always had a bag of turf on her back. I suppose in those days there were a lot of illnesses they didn't know about and crimes that went undetected.

Throughout Ireland in the nineteenth and early twentieth century the idea that you could be taken by the fairies was a very common one and there were many precautions that had to be taken to prevent it. It was particularly dangerous for babies and small children. Iron was thought to keep the wee folk away and so a mother might lay tongs across a child's cradle if she was going out of the house for a short while. In parts of South Armagh little bags of oatmeal were attached to any sort of necklace they could make and put round the children's necks and this, they believed, was effective.

Women, too, were taken and tales of this are told in many areas. The belief was so common that there was a danger that if any woman acted strangely she might be considered to be 'taken' and the efforts to 'get her back' could be tragic.

One rather bizarre story of a more fortunate case is told about a place called Dorsey McKeever, where a young mother of seven children fell ill and was dying. She passed away and the distraught children ran to tell their father in the fields. The neighbours gathered in and the day was increasingly windy. In the evening a neighbour was out working when a bottle floated through the air on a high wind. He raised his spade and with some difficulty brought it down, whereupon the dead woman emerged from the bottle alive and well. (A veritable Armagh genie!)

Everyone agreed that the wee folk had taken her and, although the bottle was being blown towards the fairy fort, the spell was broken when it was brought to earth by the spade. The neighbours accompanied her back to the house where the husband and children were mourning her and, when they looked in the death bed, there was nothing but an old black stick! The original teller of this tale claimed to know the people it happened to very well.

However, the outcome is not always so fortunate and the fairies also had a reputation for being vindictive. A story heard in County Armagh, but in many other counties as well, is told about a woman who acted as midwife to the fairies. The story was told by the woman's neighbour, who said that one night a very small man came on horseback to her neighbour to ask her if she would come and help out with the birth of his child. He took her up unto the horse and they went off, in what direction the midwife couldn't tell, but they arrived and she helped out with the birth. All went well and she was given oil to rub onto the child. She rubbed one of her own eyes and must have had oil on her fingers but she didn't realise that until later. The job done she was handsomely paid and left back to her home.

Several days later she was at the market in Castleblaney (a town not far away in the neighbouring county) and she was pleased to see the man whose child she had delivered. She asked him how his wife and child were and said how strange it was that she could see him through only one of her eyes. 'Which one?' he asked and when she told him, he stuck his finger into the eye and blinded her. (Well I did say they were unpredictable, didn't I?)

Yet there were happier incidents of people being 'away with the fairies', like Mary Jane McCormick, who was said to be a changeling. She had previously lived in the house of the man who told the story about her, and he said she was a very small woman who had a husband and son of normal size. She must have been some class of a changeling if the account is correct because every night she flew out the back window to take part in the fairy revels in the nearby fort and people coming past the spot late at night heard the wee folk calling out to her!

The 'gentry' were said to do their washing in wee pots in Segahan river and fairy pipes and one of their little silver shoes was found.

According to one account, a man who lived near their fort had a great lust for hunting and one night the fairy folk sent hounds to lure him out. He tramped the whole country after the hounds and ended up in the fort, where the fairy dwellers thrashed him soundly so that he never ever went hunting again. These fairy folk seem to have pervaded the countryside of County Armagh in an uneasy coexistence with the natives. They were the focus of a great deal of fear and consequently superstition and yet they held out a hope of favour and fortune and, like most things without explanation, they were associated with old magic. However, unless some surviving branch of their race in Wales rigs up the eggshells and sails back to Ireland, it looks like we will now have to survive without them!

> If iver ye meet the wee people at night, jist say till yerself, 'Fair may ye come an' fair may ye go with your heels to us' an' mebbe they'll pass ye by.

THE CONFERENCE OF HARES

Hunting hares was a common thing in the past but many stories were told about it – strange stories; stories about hares not being affected by gunshot or of them running off after they had been shot, leaving a trail of blood behind them. Sometimes the person who shot the hare followed them to finish the job off or, if they thought there was something odd about the hare, they might follow out of curiosity.

That's where the accounts grow very odd, for the hare eventually entered some house in the locality – that of a neighbour or a stranger, and when the hunter knocked on the door and asked to speak to the owner, the woman of the house was inevitably mysteriously injured, or simply 'unwell', and often couldn't or wouldn't put in an appearance.

Indeed many people felt that there was something other-worldly about the hare. There were those who wouldn't harm one out of a kind of respect and it was commonly believed in the farming community that it was unlucky to shoot a hare. People will tell you about the terrible cry of a wounded hare. 'It's just like a baby crying,' I've heard a man say with some distress. Of course there were also those who thought that that was all a load of balderdash.

Jim was one of the latter. I got his story from Patricia Kennedy (Autumn 2013). He was a young man in his twenties from Armagh City who had a close affinity with nature. That didn't preclude him, however, from fishing and hunting hares and rabbits. He liked nothing better than to set off with his friends in the early morning and spend the whole day fishing or chasing rabbits. If he caught any rabbits, he would arrive home in the evening with them slung over his shoulder and they would be cleaned and skinned and cooked for dinner the next day. In this way he helped to put food on the table in a family where food wasn't plentiful. Then there were the whole days that he spent

fishing. When hunger got the better of him, he would light a
fire with sticks and gather a ball of clay which he moistened with
water from the river. This he patted around the fish and placed it
in under the sticks of the fire so that the fish cooked enclosed in
its own little earthen oven. It took over half an hour and when he
extracted it, he only had to tap the clay for it to fall apart and the
cooked fish was delicious.

Jim hunted wood pigeon, which the farmers were happy
about because they ate their crops and so they didn't mind the

odd hunter coming on their land; he hunted hares too, in spite
of his mother's disapproval. She was very unhappy about this and
claimed that hares were special creatures and should be treated as
such and not harmed. To shoot one, she said, was like shooting a
human being. Jim laughed at her superstition.

Then one morning he woke shortly after dawn – much earlier
than usual. It was a fine morning and rather than go back to
sleep, he thought he'd hit the road and head for the fields and
woods to see what he could bring home. He headed out on
the Killylea Road – the route they usually took, out past the
Navan Fort. A few miles further on, he turned to the right across
the fields and made for a small wood. As he came through a gap
in the hedge to enter a field that sloped up to a kind of mound,
he saw a sight that stopped him in his tracks. He stood stock still,
trying to make sense of what was before him. The gun that he had
instinctively reached for now hung loose and redundant. A group
of hares were all standing on their back legs in the field; they were
gathered in a circle around a single hare and they were slowly
shuffling in what looked bizarrely like a slow dance around the
hare in the middle, which was also on its back legs. John couldn't
believe his eyes and he watched them for what seemed like ten
minutes. Suddenly the hare in the centre turned its head and
looked at him – stared coolly at him – and all the others then
turned too. They seemed totally aware of his presence but not in
the least frightened by him. They made no attempt to run away,
in fact they didn't budge and appeared unconcerned. Then they
got down off their hind legs, still looking at him. They parted the
circle and hopped away at a leisurely pace, with the central hare
the last to leave. He watched them make their way up the slope
of the field and, unnerved enough as he was, he actually gasped
in surprise when they stopped at the top of the mound and gave
him one last gaze.

It was a very thoughtful young man who wended his way home
that evening. It had been for all the world like a hare conference

or lecture and he had the uncanny feeling that he had just entered into another world in which he had felt like an intruder. Part of him had wanted to flee but he had been rooted to the spot by the strangeness of it all. He was unnaturally quiet that evening at home. His mother repeatedly asked him what was wrong but she couldn't get a word out of him. Finally he succumbed and told her.

'Didn't I tell you, son, you should never touch a hare. That's a wee ritual that hares have. I told you that they're special creatures. And you were honoured to see it.' He didn't laugh at her this time. He took the cartridges out of the gun and hung it up and never hunted hares again. It was years before he told anyone else because there had been something kind of sacred about the experience. In a way he felt privileged to have been allowed to witness their ritual. His mother was right; it was an honour.

Before decimalisation, Irish coins bore the images of animals. It was the poet W.B. Yeats, then a member of the senate, who recommended this. A hare was one of the animals and its image was on the thrupence.

7

GHOSTS OF THE PAST

FOOTSTEPS IN THE DEAD OF NIGHT

A woman told me that her grandfather was going home late one night from his work in Loudan the Undertakers. He was heading in the direction of Gas Lane and took a shortcut up Abbey Street. At the top of Abbey Street, opposite the Old Infirmary (now the Irish Studies Library), he heard footsteps behind him. He looked round and there was no one there so he thought it best to quicken his step. As soon as he did, the steps behind him came faster too so he got nervous and broke into a run. Whatever was behind him began to run too. He changed direction and instead of going down by the triangle (a place where an underground passage leads towards the Old Cathedral) to Callan Street, he ran straight on, right round to Castle Street, and as soon as he got to the top of Castle Street the footsteps stopped. He never took that route home again.

Of course those were sinister footsteps but a musician in the Loughgall area used to go out walking the country roads and lanes at all hours of the night. Like many performers it took him several hours to wind down after playing at a dance or concert and he enjoyed the peace and quiet of the dark, or maybe moonlit, roads.

One night as he walked along what he called 'the top road' he heard a sound like a click right behind him. He looked round and found no one there. He walked on and it started up again. It was almost like an echo of his footsteps, but he had walked this road many times and he knew there was no echo. He sped up (just like the man in the last account) and he got a sickening feeling as the sounds behind him sped up too. He stopped and it stopped and he could feel the hairs on the back of his neck begin to rise. He had walked these roads many nights and had never experienced fear but he did now.

He contemplated running flat out for home but he made himself stop and consider. He thought of the poet W.H. Davies having said that he never had anything to fear from the supernatural, it was the natural that gave him the problem. He made himself walk on at a normal pace but he knew if he had let himself run he would probably have broken his own door down in a panic to get into his house.

As it was he slowly worked out that the new laces on his shoes had a little metal toggle on the ends and that the 'click' was the metallic echo that came a fraction of a beat after his own footsteps. Had he run for home that night, he said, he would forever more be convinced that it was a ghost but, thanks to Mr Davies, he found an explanation!

BALEER

A haunting occurred in the first half of the twentieth century near the townland of Baleer. A doctor came home from South-West England to live in his aunt's house after she died. He had inherited her large house and land but what should have been a pleasant inheritance for him turned into a burden.

He could find no peace in the house and he felt constantly uneasy. He didn't see spirits or hear noises but no matter where he went in the house he felt troubled and couldn't settle. Although he wasn't of the same persuasion as the priest in nearby Keady, he went to seek his advice. I suppose there is a limited number of people who will entertain the idea of the existence of ghosts at all, so that someone who is troubled by them will seek out any sympathetic ear.

Well apparently this priest helped him so much in the exorcism of whatever was causing the unease in the house, that the good doctor donated an organ to his church in Keady – even though it wasn't his own church! The organ was replaced many years later but it seems the one in question bore a plaque saying that it was donated by a Dr Leeper.

Another thing that happened in Baleer is that a man was riding on his bicycle past my uncle's farm one night. He saw an inexplicable, ghastly white shape beside a little outhouse in the field. Now he knew the countryside very well and had often passed this field before and never seen anything like this spectre so he was alarmed.

Like the rest of us have done, he tried to curb his imagination and get the image out of his mind but the following night he had a sick feeling when he saw it again. He lingered a little because he wanted to be absolutely sure of what he was seeing so that no one would make him feel stupid by pointing out it was only an old sheet or something of that ilk. But when it moved toward him and made an unearthly sound he nearly fell off his bicycle and couldn't get away quickly enough.

He appealed to my uncle, who didn't take him seriously, but a neighbour was very disturbed because he had to pass the place every night and said that it was really no laughing matter so my uncle had to give it some thought. Uncle John finally worked out what it might be and went off to check it out. One of his sows was ready to have a litter and had disappeared and he knew that they were prone to forage about until they'd find a spot that suited them and sure enough, when he went to the same field, he found that she had taken up residence by an old outhouse. So the man was no more troubled by the ghostly swine!

THE PHANTOM COACHMAN

This story was recalled in a wonderful local history project organised by Eileen McCourt in St Patrick's Grammar School (1988).

The story of the Phantom Coachman of Greenpark is a very long-standing one in Armagh. Greenpark was a primary school which the Christian Brothers started in 1852. The Brothers, not men renowned for their fantasy, experienced strange happenings in and around the old house that they were trying to put into shape.

The house had been built in the 1750s and was known to be haunted. It had been occupied, at one point, by a retired army captain who had not only killed his daughter but had taken his own life too. This was thought to be the reason for the haunting. During the night a carriage was heard to drive up to the hall door. There was loud knocking on the door and then footsteps passed through the hall. Up the stairs they went, turned right and went into a back room.

It seems that on a few occasions the noises at night were so bad that the Brothers, not renowned for their delicate sensibilities, had to leave the house in the middle of the night and go out unto the lawns. The Church authorities were informed and a procession of exorcism was made through the whole house and out around the boundaries of the property. Since then there have been no more disturbances but the mystique of the haunting still fires the imagination of pupils and has developed into the story of the ubiquitous headless coachman.

THE ROAD TO THE NAVAN

Strange things seemed to happen in one particular area on the road from Armagh City to the Navan Fort. At one time there was a cluster of dwellings and there was one house in particular which is still talked about. They say that house was cursed. It finally burned down, but that was the last of a series of mishaps that befell people who lived in it.

The story goes that around the early 1900s, a poor woman couldn't pay her rent and she and her family were put out by the landlord. Before she left she knelt down and 'prayed a curse' on the place – wishing ill-luck to anyone who would take it over after her. And by all accounts her 'praying' was effective.

I knew of one couple who moved into it after their honeymoon. Two of their children were born there and after that they managed to find another place because they never felt they had luck in it. Indeed they were very keen to leave, especially because one morning their father had gone out to find the cattle lying dead – inexplicably.

When the next family lived there, the husband went out one morning to find his horse dead on the road – once again inexplicably.

Another man had a shop near there. One day his daughter slipped on Leger Hill. After that she didn't grow anymore and stayed in the house. She was always there when people went to visit and everyone knew her. She was a diminutive person, well liked, but rightly or wrongly, everyone felt that the curse on the place had brought about her hardship and disability.

Then a brewery was built in the same place and when, in time, it fell into disrepair, stone was taken from it to build a garage. A car went across the road by the garage killing a young girl. Once again there was no explanation. It became known as 'brewery corner' and was reputed to be the haunt of ghosts.

All those who knew the ins and outs of the stories of the ghosts have sadly passed away now so we shall never come by the finer details of the hauntings – unless they return to tell us of course. The names of the families mentioned above *are* known though and it would seem that the reputation of the place really did have some justification.

PERSONAL GHOST STORIES

The Moy Road

John was driving out the Moy Road one dark rainy night. In spite of the wipers it was difficult to see through the windscreen. A car was coming from the opposite direction driving towards Armagh at a place called Allistragh. Suddenly a man stepped out in front of John's car. He seemed to come from nowhere. John slammed on the brakes but he'd had no warning whatsoever. There was just no way to avoid him the way he'd stepped right into the path of his car and he hadn't even noticed him at the side of the road. He jumped out of the car in a panic and ran round to the front to see how he was. The other car stopped too and the man got out and came over.

'How is he? Did you hit him? Is he badly hurt?' he asked, but John was looking around him bewildered.

'I can't see him. Can you?' John asked.

'He must be under the car,' the other driver said and they both searched all round and under the car.

'You might have knocked him into the ditch.' They both hurried to the ditch in spite of the driving rain, because they knew they'd have to get him to hospital. There was no one at all at the side of the road. They scoured the place but there was no sign of anyone.

'But he has to be here somewhere,' John said. 'He walked right in front of the car. He was wearing a jacket – not dressed for the rain at all. Did you see him?'

'I did surely. You couldn't have avoided him the way he walked out in front of you.'

'Well good God, where is he now?' John was confused. 'What'll we do? Should I report it to the police?'

'Well it's like this,' the other man said. 'There's no one here now. I can't understand it. I've never seen anything like it.'

'You did see him?' John asked again, getting a bit desperate. 'Like, it wasn't my imagination or anything?'

'Not at all,' the other man reassured him, 'sure I seen him too. It's a terrible, dirty oul' night, but I seen him as plain as anything. You may go on up the road for there's nothin' nor nobody here.'

'Do you think it was … ? I've never seen a ghost; I wouldn't know what it looked like,' said John.

'Me neither,' said the other man, 'but I seen him and he's not here now, so … God knows. Come on man, we're getting wet. You'll be foundered. Get into your car and drive on and good luck to you.'

John was badly shaken. He got into the car and slowly started it up. He drove on to the Moy to see his friends but he left their company early. As he drove back home that night he slowed down at the spot but nothing crossed his path this time. He couldn't wait to get into his own house and it really helped him when he was able to recount the whole thing to his wife. It was the worst fright he'd ever had in his life.

Late-Night Visitors

Another time that footsteps were heard was when Hugh, who was about twenty at the time, was asked to take his turn at sleeping in the room with his grandfather, who wasn't that long off death. His aunt, who looked after him, was weary with the constant care she gave him. She was delighted not to be on call that night and went to bed secure in the knowledge that Hugh would be at hand should her father need anything during the night. The grandfather was already in bed and Hugh eventually made his way through the sleeping house and up the stairs to the bedroom. His grandfather was sleeping peacefully – well his snores didn't bode well for Hugh getting a peaceful sleep but he was glad the old man was able to get his rest and wasn't suffering any pain. He quietly undressed in the light from the landing so as not to waken him, then he closed the bedroom door and slid under the heavy blankets of the bed. Just as he was acclimatising himself to the snores, he heard footsteps on the stairs. Now he knew there was only his aunt in the house and that she was asleep; moreover, the sound was of more than one set of feet. In the normal run of things he was a brave young man and he wasn't prone to imaginings either but when he heard them reach the door of the bedroom and heard the sound of the door handle, he found himself slipping down under the bedclothes.

Someone – two people – had come into the room. His grandfather seemed to have woken up and was talking in a very companionable way to whoever it was. Hugh could hear that there was a two-way conversation going on. It lasted for about ten minutes and he thought they would never stop for he was nearly smothered in his hidey hole. He had no intention, however, of coming up for air, because he knew for certain that there was absolutely no one in the vicinity who would go visiting this sick old man in the middle of the night and he was scared and bewildered at the odd situation he found himself in. His grandfather sounded remarkably animated and Hugh felt like a total outsider in his little lair. Farewells were being exchanged now and he heard the door open and close and the steps on the stair. His grandfather was out of bed and clunking about and he nearly leapt out of his skin when a heavy hand came down on the bed and shook him.

'What do you think of that pair of blades? Imagine them two ladies comin' to see me?' and he seemed delighted with himself. 'Your mother and that cousin of hers! Hard to credit it!'

Hugh's mother had died when he was nine years old. He had his work cut out for him getting the old man back to bed and settled down but he, himself, couldn't sleep for a long time afterwards. He didn't know what to think. It was the strangest thing he'd ever experienced and he often talked about it throughout his life. It wasn't long after that that his grandfather died.

Hugh too has passed on now; it was his brother who told me the story of the late night visitors.

Sounds in the Night

On the outskirts of Armagh lives a woman I know quite well. When she was about seven, she heard her father come in one night – he wasn't often out late but he'd gone to some event that night. She heard him come in through the door, bank up the Raeburn stove with slack for the night and go into the kitchen to make himself a cup of tea. About ten minutes later she heard the same procedure all over again and was quite puzzled by it. Her father was quite definitely in the house the second time so she wondered had he really come in at all the first time. She gradually came to realise that when she heard this happen it was like an auditory premonition she was having. Soon she was able to gauge her father's homecomings because she would always hear him come in between five to ten minutes before his actual arrival. She also heard heavy treads or thumps on the stairs like a person going up or down; her friends, when they stayed over, heard it too and there were unpleasant stories as to how the previous resident had met his end. Yet she said these things never bothered her. They didn't scare her in any way; she just accepted them and as a child didn't think that much about them.

A Jocular Poltergeist

I've heard horrendous stories about poltergeists, as I'm sure you have too. It's not a subject to be taken lightly and most people won't speak of them because their experience or that of their friends or acquaintances has been so disturbing. What a relief it is then to hear about a jocular poltergeist! I didn't even know such a thing existed until my brother told me that he had called in to see a woman he knew, who lived on The Mall in Armagh.

'She went off to make me a cup of tea,' he said, 'and I heard her speaking to someone, so I thought there was another person in the house, but she continued to say the occasional thing to this other person when she was in the room with me. She called him "Jack", and he didn't bother her in the least but it seems he was always playing tricks on her – moving things. For instance, if she put the cup and saucer down, she'd turn round to find it at the other side of the table, or if she hung up a coat, it would end up on a different hook so that she'd have difficulty finding things. She talked away to this "Jack" reprimanding him for moving things and playing pranks. "Stop that, Jack," she'd say, or "Behave yourself now, Jack!" It seemed that she was quite content to have his company because she lived alone.' What a lovely thought: a friendly ghost! And you wondered why you kept losing things in your house!?

The Gift

I've spoke of auditory experiences but a woman from the Navan Street vicinity had visual sightings. She became troubled by the fact that she could see people who were dead and consulted a priest when she was about twenty years old. He told her that she had been born with one foot in this world and one in the other and that it was a gift.

'It's a gift I'd rather not have, Father,' she said.

'Well you have it now, so just accept it,' he replied.

Her first memory of one of these 'experiences' was when her granny lay dying in the room next to her bedroom. She was in bed at night when she saw her grandmother come through the wall of the next room and smile and say goodbye to her. A short while later her father opened the bedroom door and said, 'Your granny has just died.'

'I know,' she said.

'Sure how could you know?' he asked.

'She just came out of the wall to say goodbye a wee while ago,' she replied with the innocence of a young child.

When she was a little older she told her mother about this 'gift' and quoted the above incident as the first time she'd experienced it.

'Oh, you had it before that,' her mother said. 'I saw it when you were a baby.' And she went on to tell her about the time when, as a toddler, she had developed a raging fever and the mother was so concerned that she sent for the doctor even though they had to pay for a doctor to visit the house. People never locked their front door in those days and her mother was so worried about her that she stayed in the bedroom upstairs because, as she said, 'You were burning up with the fever and I was afraid I was going to lose you. I heard someone come in downstairs so I was relieved that the doctor had arrived and I heard her come up the stairs as I knew she would. From where I was sitting beside the cot I heard the bedroom door knob turn and the door began to open. I turned to greet the doctor and there was no one there but the door was open wide. Then you sat up in the cot and smiled and reached out your arms as though someone was coming towards you.

Shortly afterwards the doctor came in downstairs and I called to her. She came up the stairs and examined you but she said you'd recovered and couldn't understand why I'd been at my wit's end about you. I'll never forget it. I knew then that there was something a bit different about you.'

8

LOCAL LORE

MASTER MCGRATH

Paterson gives a good account of the history of the dog in Harvest Home *and of course the* Lurgan Mail *and many other newspapers carried accounts of all his successes. I am indebted to Jim Blaney for the anecdotes about the Liar Kelly.*

Perhaps the strongest folk memory in Lurgan is that of Master McGrath. In 1610, O'Neilland was granted to John Brownlow by the Crown. In 1616 his son William succeeded him and is attributed with founding the town of Lurgan. It received its patent for markets and fairs in 1629. By the end of the seventeenth century it was occupied mostly by linen weavers and in 1712 they began to produce damask. That was a very important part of its history, but it is equally as well known for a dog that was bought in 1867 by Charles Brownlow, commonly known as Lord Lurgan.

Master McGrath was a very unprepossessing greyhound. It was owned by a Mr Galway in Dungarvan, County Waterford. Galway's trainer, John Harney, had given some of his master's greyhound pups to Thomas Ducey to rear. Ducey had put this particular

pup in the charge of his young nephew. Like any young boy who
spends long hours walking and feeding a dog, he had grown fond
of it to the extent that he could even ignore it's less than handsome
appearance. 'It had an ugly little head, and a little tail, which was
more like a rat's …' The dog had been named Master McGrath
after the young boy so he was devastated to hear that Mr Galway
was disappointed in the dog and that it would be drowned.

When the trainer John Harney called on Ducey to see how
the pups were progressing he heard how downcast the boy was
at the thought of his little pup being done away with. Harney
himself had found it hard to understand why the dog was not
more promising since it had such a good pedigree. He was bred
from Lady Sarah – renowned for her tenacity, and Dervock, a
dog noted for his speed. 'The Master', whelped in 1866, was the
runt of the litter and definitely the worst looking. Seeing the boy's
disappointment, Harney postponed his decision and determined
to train it himself for a few weeks to see if it was worth lifting the
awful sentence.

Mr Galway was very friendly with Lord Lurgan, who held
great coursing carnivals at Lurgan Castle. In 1867 Galway sent
him a leash of greyhounds, among which was the young dog
in question and Harney sent him off with the instructions that
he should be entered for the Visitors Cup. The Visitors Cup
was one of the important events in the carnival and it was open
to the many visitors and guests who came to the castle for it.
It took place in October and Master McGrath performed well

in the first two rounds, he led by three lengths in the third and to everyone's amazement the 'ugly little dog' beat the favourite, What's the Tip, in the final. This was but the first of many times he would bring wonder and joy to his followers, and great excitement to the spectators.

The following week he led four terrific trials. He was described by an observer who watched him chasing the hare:

> His eyes were like two living balls of fire. The muscles of his back sprung and twitched like whalebone. The dog looked as if he were supercharged with electricity. I knew at once that the hare had no chance. McGrath swept round her when she broke, and crashed into his game as if shot from a gun. I can never forget it.
>
> (T.G.F. Paterson, *Harvest Home* (Dundalk: Dundalgan Press, 1975), p. 78)

An old greyhound trainer who was familiar with him described him as having 'a sour-looking plainish head. He looked at you as if he owned the universe.' He went on to describe his very neat legs and feet that had two white toes on each. These matched the 'long white streak on his chest and a small white patch over one of his shoulders' and then there was the tail that he hardly had at all – it was so short and fine. 'Over his back he was ticked with white, as if a shower of hail fell on him.'

In 1868 he was entered for the most prestigious event in the coursing world, the Waterloo Cup, and after a shaky start he ran shoulder to shoulder with the favourite until he managed to pull ahead of her but then Lobelia caught up with him and it was in the final moments that The Master streaked forward to make a decisive win. It was the first time the Waterloo Cup had been won by a dog from Ireland so of course it caused a great stir.

That October he performed well in the Brownlow Cup, running against thirty-two other dogs. In 1869 his stakes were 6 to 1 in the Waterloo Cup. He was in against Borealis – a dog with a great reputation. They both left the other dogs far behind but when Master McGrath outstripped Borealis by eight lengths the crowd couldn't believe their eyes. They had never seen such speed. Then Lobelia was back to try and steal his crown and at first it looked like she might but then The Master, like one demented, took the lead and drove home to the finish. In the final he had to contend with the Scottish 'Bab-at-the-Bowster', a hound that had won many accolades during that year. The crowd held its breath as the two battled it out in a race of great suspense but Master McGrath was in at the kill as ever.

In 1870 he was back at the Altcar course near Liverpool, but the weather there was dreadful. There were sixty-four dogs running and the betting stakes began at 7 to 2 but on the morning of the race they were down to 3 to 1. A hard frost was beginning to lift and the thawing conditions left the course perilous. At one point The Master lost his footing and consequently his stride, leaving his supporters in an agony of anticipation and then he followed the hare to the river and the ice cracked, plunging him into icy water. His trainer Wilson raced to the rescue and wrapped him up. It was the end of his career everyone thought, including his owner Lord Lurgan, but nursed by Wilson he came through it and was raring to go again in his sixth year. He won all round him in the Brownlow Cup.

It was, however, with considerable apprehension that they brought him to Liverpool once again. The stories of his feats had spread all over. He had developed such a tremendous reputation that people came from far and wide to see him. With all he had to live up to, a failure would be such a shame. The tension was high amid the crowds that flocked to the course.

Master McGrath had never run better. The final came and it was a dog called Pretender that was his rival – an apt name for one who would try to steal his crown. From the outset The Master ran with such determined stride that the crowd went with him in their hearts. They knew he'd do it and satisfaction was theirs as well as his. They were there running with him as he finished

that race and they were there receiving the Waterloo Cup for the
third time with him. They felt that his victory was their victory.
No doubt his mother, Lady Sarah, and his father, Dervock, were
with him all the way too, looking down on him from some canine
paradise in the sky!

The *Armagh Guardian* newspaper reported in 1871: 'Master
McGrath was brought to Windsor Castle by desire of the Queen
where he was petted and made much of by the Royal family.'

He died two years after his great Waterloo Cup triumph, having
lost only one out of the thirty-seven courses he ran: a record
unsurpassed. He put Lurgan on the map and Lurgan put a statue
of him in the town. Dungarvan, where he was whelped, put up a
statue to him too. S.H. Aughnacloy wrote a lovely description of
his funeral in the *John O'London* newspaper, in 1946:

> The funeral was a most touching scene. In front of Brownlow
> Castle at Lurgan is a large green sward, at the left of which is a
> small wicket gate. When the dog was to be buried the tenants
> and retainers of the Brownlow Estate gathered together, each man
> with a greyhound in leash. Slowly each one passed in through
> the little wicket gate, across the main hall entrance, where
> Lord Lurgan stood, circled round the lawn and round the little
> oaken coffin placed in the middle of it, pausing for a moment at
> the coffin. So out again by the same little gate, while the trainer
> carried the coffin away to be buried in the laurels some few yards
> away in the shrubbery.

This wasn't quite as contrived as it might seem; I've heard of
horses coming one by one, of their own accord and to the surprise
of their owner to pay their respects to a horse that was dying in
the field they all shared.

The following song was composed as a tribute to Master
McGrath and is still sung today:

O'eighteen sixty eight being the date and the year
Those Waterloo sportsmen and more did appear
For to gain the great prizes and bear them awa'
Never counting on Ireland and Master McGrath.

On the twelfth of November, that day of renown
McGrath, his keeper they left Lurgan Town
A gale in the Channel it soon drove them o'er
On the thirteenth they landed on England's fair shore.

Oh, but when they arrived there in big London Town
Those great English sportsmen all gathered 'round
And one of those gentlemen standing nearby
Said, 'Is that the great dog you call Master McGrath?'

Oh, well one of those gentlemen standing around
Said, 'I don't care a damn for your Irish greyhound'
And another he sneered with a scornful 'Ha ha'
We'll soon humble the pride of your Master McGrath.

Oh, McGrath he looked up and he wagged his old tail
Informing his lordship, 'Sure I know what you mean
Don't fear noble Brownlow, don't fear them a gra'
We'll soon tarnish their laurels,' says Master McGrath.

Oh, well Rose stood uncovered, that great English pride
Her master and keeper were close by her side
They let them away and the crowd cried, 'Hurrah'
For the pride of all England and Master McGrath.

Oh, well Rose and the Master they both ran along
'I wonder', said Rose, 'What took you from your home?
You should have stayed there in your Irish domain
And not come to gain laurels on Albion's plain.'

'Well I know' says the Master, 'We have wild heather bogs
But, bedad, in old Ireland there's good men and dogs
Lead on, bold Britannia, give none of your jaw
Stuff that up your nostrils', says Master McGrath.

Well, the hare she led on just as swift as the wind
He was sometimes before her and sometimes behind
He jumped on her back and held up his old paw
Three cheers for old Ireland and Master McGrath.

This greyhound became so much part of the psyche of Lurgan that nearly 150 years later its citizens still speak of it. Probably because of the dog's reputation, a greyhound racetrack – Celtic Park – was built on the Portadown Road coming out of Lurgan, but it was subsequently closed down. Influential members of the town disapproved of this recreational activity taking place on a Sunday because of the gambling associated with it. In fact, up to the 1980s, Northern Ireland was quiet as the grave on Sundays because certain religions thought that the only fitting activity on a Sunday was church-going, with the result that even swings in playgrounds were tied up on the Lord's Day.

This, however, didn't stop the seed and breed of greyhounds being discussed during the week in the pubs of Lurgan. Someone who was listened to with great attention was 'The Liar Kelly', who was well known around the 1950s. This epithet was far from derogatory; people regarded The Liar with a mixture of awe and amusement, not to mention amazement. 'Wondrous statements' rather than 'hyperbole' would be the best way to describe Kelly's fabrications. His stories were notorious and he provided the people of Lurgan with great entertainment and when he entered the public house they eagerly awaited his pronouncements. Such was the force of Kelly's personality, though, that no matter how outrageous his accounts were, no one dared laugh in his presence. The result was that he was almost as entertaining when he wasn't there for once he had left they used to crack up laughing.

He came into the pub one night and joined two men at the bar as they argued about the relative merit of different grey-hounds and their own in particular. Each man was bragging about the speed and ability of his own greyhound. Of course they were aware of the fact that Kelly would find a way to outdo all their boasts but they were stopped in their tracks when he declared:

'I have the best bitch in the world!'

'In the world?!' they chorused.

'In the world,' he replied.

'How do you make that out?' they asked.

'Well,' he said, 'I entered her for the two-thirty race and before the other dogs were right out of the traps, she was half way round the track!'

'No! Are you serious?' they asked.

'But what do you think happened then?' he went on. 'She lay down and whelped two pups.'

'What!' gasped the two men, hardly able to believe their ears.

'And would you believe she got up again and finished the race! She came in first and what do you think but the two pups came in second and third!' – no laughter but a few choked pints.

The two men weren't above egging Kelly on or trying to put him into a corner: 'And what became of her?' one of them asked.

'Och, she died,' said Kelly. 'I had it skinned and they made a waistcoat out of it – the loveliest waistcoat you ever did see.'

Around 1947 there was a terrible frost and Lurgan Lake – the old Brownlow Estate had come into public possession as Lurgan Park – was frozen over. There was a huge crowd in the park. The majority were sliding on the lake but those who were well enough off to own skates were skating. Kelly described to his pub mates how he had gone to the quieter side of the lake to get some peace away from the crowds.

'Then what happened? I fell through a hole where the ice had cracked and what do you think? It was three days before I could find it again to get out.'

On another occasion people were vying for the biggest rat they had ever seen.

'It was huge,' said one. 'It was at least 2ft long!'

'That's nothing,' said Kelly. 'I was at the quarry last week and I saw the biggest rat that was ever heard tell of. It was that big I knew no one would believe it, so I took my hanky out of my pocket and I put it round its neck and walked it into town [about a half a mile away]. And when I got to the head of the plain [the local expression for the top end of Francis Street], its tail was only leaving the quarry!'

The Liar Kelly too is dead and gone, but not forgotten.

THE BULLETS

Since Dermot Hicks's excellent little book Road Bowls in Armagh *(1973), edited by Fr Murray, there has been an ever-increasing number of books published about 'the bullets':* Road Bowling in Ireland *(1996) by Brian Toal and Fintan Lane's* Long Bullets: A History of Road Bowling in Ireland *(2005) are but a few I dipped into. Mgr Murray, a keen follower of the sport, told me about how it had developed in recent years and there's a good historical account in Paterson's* Harvest Home.

The Armagh Bullet Throwers are legendary! 'Bullets' is a game peculiar to Armagh and has frequently been open to misinterpretation, especially during the not so distant 'Troubles'. People referring to 'playing bullets' often leave outsiders, who don't know of the game, a little anxious. The official title is 'Road Bowling' and it was played in some eleven counties in Ireland in the past, where it was usually called 'long bullets', but in the recent past it has been very much the preserve of the two counties of Armagh and Cork. In Cork the sport is known as 'Bouling' and both counties have a fiercely supportive following. Important contests attract thousands of supporters.

The idea in Bullets is to play along fairly flat roads and see who can throw the bowl or bullet the furthest. The 'ball' is a 28oz iron bowl; in the past it could have weighed up to 6 pounds and at one time was made of stone. The game is played over a 3-mile course and the winner is the player who completes it in the least number

of throws or shots. A game or 'score' is usually played with two contestants.

The player is accompanied by a second known as a 'road shower' or 'handler' who stands, legs apart, between 50 to 80 yards away in the direction the player is aiming and the thrower tries to make the bowl run between this man's legs. It serves to give him a point of focus. The equivalent of the handler might be the caddy in golf but road bowling is a much more visceral game.

While strength in the player counts for something it by no means guarantees success because co-ordination is the key thing and the speed of the run before the throw is crucial. This is well illustrated by Skelton's description of feeling overconfident in his ability to beat a challenger – a man he discounted on account of his puny physique. He was dismayed when this 'little' man threw the bowl twice as far as him.

Although in the past it was a sport played by both religions in the community, when the focus moved away from playing on Saturday to Sunday play many Protestants, unfortunately, dropped out and it became exclusively Catholics who played.

There are few people from Armagh who don't have memories of sitting in cars on summer or autumn evenings, or particularly on a Sunday afternoon, waiting with infinite patience for the bullet scout to wave them on. They might have to wait for five, ten or more minutes while a throw took place and yet the drivers rarely complained. The scouts, of course, are very necessary because it could, potentially, be very dangerous, though considering the lethal nature and speed of the ball, they have a very good safety record.

As far back as 1741 there is mention of the fact that in Derry the playing of Long Bullets on the ramparts was an offence which would incur a hefty fine, and the Summary Jurisdiction Act of 1851 declared it an offence to play games on the public highway. Right up to the 1960s the game was officially illegal but it rather depended on the whim of the individual officer with what rigour the law was applied.

The bullet players of early times were folk legends and are still remembered as such. The first well-recorded hero of the game in County Armagh was Jim Macklin, who made his name in the late nineteenth century. He was said to be a great all-round athlete who could do a long jump of 23ft. They say he would jump over two cart horses for the prize of a pint of beer (that's desperation for you!). He could jump in and out of a barrel, and over a half-door and back without hitting his head. One Friday night he was coming home from the Moy Fair after he had drunk a considerable amount and he took it into his head to jump the canal lock at Blackwatertown, a town 7 miles outside Armagh City. The lock is 11ft across with a concrete block on either side. When reports of this feat got out the unbelievers challenged him to do it again before witnesses on the following Sunday. Not only did he repeat the task but he did a turn in mid-air to land facing them – taking his bow so to speak! His reputation at throwing bullets was such that they say the only way he could get a gamble was by throwing the bullet under his leg!

Jim Curran was a blacksmith from Salter's Grange in County Armagh. His reputation as a player combined with his occupation gave rise to him being called 'The Hammerman Curran'. He was usurped, however, in the 1920s by Peter Donnelly, who was eventually referred to simply as 'The Hammerman'. Dan Gribben, who preceded him, was such a good thrower that it was said 'he could cush off a docken leaf' ('cush' meaning to bounce or deflect). He was noted for coming from behind to perform a stunning finish, usually winning the accolades.

Armagh and Cork have two distinct styles of bowling. Armagh have an underarm throw whereby the player releases the ball after a run of maybe thirty yards and they put a spin on the metal ball to negotiate corners. Cork players, on the other hand, bowl overarm. After a run of about ten yards they swing the arm over and back to release the ball from the hip ('hinch') and they clear the corners by lobbing or 'lofting' the bowl into the air and over the hedges and trees – a style developed because it was impossible to predict the run of the ball over the very bad roads that existed at one time in County Cork. For their part, Armagh players are skilled at reading the fall and surface of the road and taking advantage of it. Mick Barry, a Cork 'bouling' hero, managed to hit the Cork Viaduct – 99ft high!

Three Cork men who were working in Belfast heard about the game in Armagh and thought they could make a bit of money by bringing a good player from Cork to compete with the Armagh player Donnelly. Under the guise of having Tim Delaney working with them, they sent down to Cork for him, met him in Dublin and took him back with them to Belfast. His seconds, or handlers, made the arduous journey later in the week. They arrived in Armagh by train the following Sunday morning and the railway station was crowded because the locals wanted to see what this Cork player Tim Delaney was like. His handler, Mick O'Shea, recounted that they were not a little daunted by these Northerners. Full of curiosity the spectators lined the course that afternoon to see how Delaney would throw. Every time he tried to throw they moved in to get a good look, so much so that, after half an hour, the police had to be called in (by this illegal sport) to keep the spectators on one side of the road and let Delaney proceed with his throw! Although Donnelly played well, Delaney eventually drew ahead and his handler Jack O'Shea was alarmed when he saw the spectators crowd onto the road. He thought a fight had developed but then he discovered that it was because the Hammerman Donnelly had graciously conceded defeat and the two men were shaking hands.

It was some time after the Depression of the 1930s that Red Joe McVeigh became the next giant to dominate the local scene and he was the first Armagh man to play in Cork. His opponent was the great Mick Barry and no one expected him to win. Although the game was held in the morning to avoid a large crowd, there were 3,000 spectators there. McVeigh played a superb game and won, much to the dismay of those who hadn't considered him worth betting on. McVeigh eventually retired, but his father, Joe McVeigh Senior, is still remembered for playing a match against Frank Cullen when they were both in their seventies!

Mick Barry from Cork continued to take part in the fray and it was Danny McParland from Armagh who stepped into McVeigh's shoes. McParland dominated the northern game and threw the longest shot in bullet's history: 512 yards. He and Mick Barry battled the bit out over many years for All Ireland Titles and when he played in Cork the spectators couldn't understand how he could throw a bowl so fast without a swing (the Cork overarm style). Barry, for his part, dominated Cork bowling for twenty years. He was an incredibly dedicated player and one of his followers spoke for many others when he said, 'I've doubted me father and I've doubted me mother, but I've never doubted you Mickey Boy.'

This is but a small sample of the great road bowling heroes of the past.

In a storytelling project in a primary school in Tullysaran (a townland a few miles outside Armagh City) a wee lad came in one day with this anecdote from his grandfather:

In my great-granda's day the bullets was illegal, because if someone threw a bullet and there was a man comin' roun' the corner on his bike an' he got hit … (shrug of the shoulders) … who would pay for the arms or legs? So the police made it illegal. Well one Sunday afternoon when the men were out throwin' bullets, the police come down the hill from Armagh and the scout seen them and warned the boys. So they jumped over the ditch into my great-granda's farm and they grabbed whatever they could find: spades, rakes, pitchforks an' they started workin' an' some of them grabbed oul' buckets that had holes in them an started milkin' the cows. Then the police came intil' the farm and they says to the men, 'Were you boys throwin' bullets?'

'Not at all,' says the men. 'Can't you see we're workin' here on
this farm.'

An' the police never even noticed that the milk was goin' thru'
the holes in the buckets intil the groun'.

An' the sergeant scratched his head and says, 'A never seen as
many people workin' on a Sunday!'

The game was subsequently legalised but by all accounts the
police were indeed very keen to catch people red-handed in those
days. Apparently a certain unpopular sergeant used to lie in wait
in the long grass, ready to pounce when the players and their iron
ball appeared. The fine was 10 shillings, which was a substantial
amount of money in those days – especially if the people in
question happened to be unemployed.

One of the many little tricks – or signs of resourcefulness –
employed by players was seen when play was called off one
evening due to the failing light. It was decided to put a mark on
a nearby signpost (known locally as a 'fingerpost') to show where
the last bowl had reached so that they could continue throwing
from that point the next day. It seems that celestial beings came
during the night and miraculously moved the signpost to a more
favourable position for one of the parties. Perhaps those celestial
beings had a lot of money riding on the outcome!

Some say the game was introduced by the Dutch soldiers when
they came with William of Orange in 1681. As it was traditionally a game played by weavers, it has also been suggested that it
came in from Yorkshire with the linen workers – linen being a
very important industry in County Armagh in the eighteenth,
nineteenth and the early twentieth centuries. The game is also
played in Holland and there is a 400-year tradition of playing it
in Germany.

Paterson quotes William Wright, who wrote about the uncles
of the Brontë sisters playing bullets in 1812. Incidentally he also
claims that, while their father Patrick Brontë came from County

Down, they were probably descended from Torlagh Bronty from Armaghbrague. In addition, he notes that bullets are mentioned in a poem that Jonathan Swift wrote while staying in Markethill and it features too in the writing of Skelton, who was from Derriaghy, County Antrim.

However, in the 1950s, a club, Ból Chumann Na hÉireann, was formed and in the 1960s an All Ireland Organisation came into being and through that the sport began to find legitimacy. It gained enough respectability for the games or 'scores' to be covered by newspapers. In 1969 the first international bowling tournament was held in Losser in Holland. The game is called Klootschiessen in Germany, where the whole approach to it was a much more formal one, and, with subsequent All-Ireland and international tournaments the sport in Ireland, has become more formalised too. In the 1970s various bowling events were featured on television.

Road Bowling had always been a male preserve for both players and spectators but in the 1970s one father entered his daughter in the under-sixteen competition. His assessment of her ability proved correct and she won. By the 1980s women's involvement in the sport, which had been building up over many years, became significant and the first All-Ireland Women's Senior Championship took place in 1981.

In addition to the senior and under-18 sections, new grades of competition were added throughout the 1980s and there are now even sections for Under-14s. In 1985 the Armagh players travelled to Cork for the newly established King of the Roads Festival – it wasn't until 1996 that they added a Queen of the Roads competition. The year 1985 also saw the first World Road Bowling Championship and the 1998 one was held in Armagh. The 1990s saw a branch of Ból Chumann Éireann started in the USA, where the sport had been played sporadically by Irish emigrants. In 2004 there were branches in all four provinces of Ireland and the sport has continued to undergo a great resurgence in recent years. It's worthy of note that 10 per cent of the senior players are from the travelling community, which has long been active in road bowls.

Bullet throwing has moved away from the colourful, homespun athletes of the past and extended nearly beyond recognition. A Hall of Fame has even been established so the great champions will be 'gone but not forgotten' and both they and the early visitors from Cork will go down in the annals of Armagh.

APPLE COUNTRY

Though not exactly the Garden of Eden, County Armagh is 'coming down' with apples and is often referred to as 'apple country'. Of course apples are grown in other counties but Armagh is the acknowledged centre of the industry and it abounds with orchards. In fact Loughgall, in the north of the county, is like a foreign landscape with its weird-looking pruned trees. In May, when the apple blossom is at its best, the area is incredibly beautiful. It's also a lovely sight in October when the trees are burgeoning with fruit and the place turns into a hive of activity for the apple-picking.

The apple was regarded as a 'chieftain tree' and its presence in the county is mentioned in some old manuscripts: namely that St Patrick planted an apple tree to the east of the city. It's also on record that the Culdees, a monastic order responsible for choral services, received apples as a special treat on certain festivals. In 1155, there was an obituary held for one of the Macans who once owned these lands. The chieftain was praised for the strong drink he had his people make from their apples.

The planting of fruit trees was first made compulsory in the county in 1666. It's noted too that in 1682 'good cider' was sold in Portadown and that farmers were obliged to plant a percentage of their land in apple trees. In 1835 Armagh had a reputation for large orchards and travellers like the writer Thackeray made a note of this when he visited Armagh in 1843. By 1888 the areas around Loughgall, Richhill and Portadown were heavily populated with orchards and buyers were coming from Scotland and England. All through the twentieth century apples have been synonymous with the county. An early legend involves the son of the King of Ulster:

Baile, an Ulster prince, fell in love with Aillin, a Leinster princess. Both their parents opposed the match. The lovers were so determined in their love that an appeal was made to the druids to settle the matter. They decreed that the couple could spend eternity together but not this life. That should have been the end of the matter but forbidden lovers will often search out devious and sometimes dangerous means to meet. Through secret channels of communication they arranged a clandestine meeting at Rossnaree near the Boyne.

It's said that Baile left Emain Macha and travelled surreptitiously to what's now called Dundalk. There's an inlet there where the river Boyne flows out into the sea. He waited there on the strand for Aillin. When news reached him of her death he was overcome with grief. Aillin too was told of her lover's death but whether he was actually dead by that time, or if that was part of the same cruel plan to kill their love, I don't know. In any case she couldn't live without him either.

Tradition has it that an apple tree and a yew tree were planted on their graves. Many years later they were cut down and made into tablets, where their story and the story of other lovers was written down.

The beach on which Baile waited for Aillin became known as Traigh Baile (Gaelic for Baile's Strand) and was known as such up to medieval times, when it became known as Dundalk. Many centuries later the poet W.B. Yeats wrote a play called 'On Baile's Strand'.

Apples were always part of local Halloween celebrations. Apart from the compulsory apple tart baked with a ring, money and other trinkets, there was an apple hung by a string from the ceiling; hands were tied behind backs and you had to try to take a bite from the apple. Everyone took a turn and the person who succeeded got the apple. It wasn't much of a prize but, as a child, it was a tremendous victory. Similarly with hands tied behind backs children tried to duck their heads into a basin of cold water to retrieve an apple sitting at the bottom of it. It resulted in wet but happy and excited children.

For many in Loughgall apple-growing is a way of life and they specialise in the Bramley apple. The year is spent pruning, spreading, mowing and keeping disease at bay. Apples are picked and sold fresh to the markets and the windfalls are sent to Bulmers in Clonmel for processing into apple juice. It's a precarious occupation though, because everything depends on the weather. If the temperature should fall too low when the blossom is out, the growers could end up with no more than 15 per cent of their crop, and if there's a bad summer, it can spell disaster for them. The third Monday in September sees the harvest time if there has been sufficient sunshine to mature the fruit. For the apple picking, pickers come in from all over Europe.

There's always a supervisor to direct or check up on the proceedings. In the past they used 50lb wooden boxes for the fruit but now they have apple bins that are moved mechanically. On one occasion a supervisor found that two Canadian pickers had gone missing. They became a little concerned for them and searched the orchards only to finally come across them courting in the apple bin! Fortunately no one had emptied a hundred weight of apples in on top of them.

As well as the Red Russetts and Beauty of Bath and all the regular names of apples, there were the Blood of the Boyne and the No Surrenders. The latter were sought by the hawkers who went to Derry to sell their wares on what was known as 'Derry Day' on 12 August. It's more widely known as The Apprentice Boys March.

This landscape of Loughgall is etched with political strife – as bitter as the apple blossom is breathtakingly beautiful. The lanes, fields and trees still bear names going back to The Battle of the Yellow Ford (1598) when Bagnall was defeated by O'Neill in a very rare native victory. Hugh O'Neill, obviously a highly skilled tactician, lured Bagnall's troops into the local bogs and O'Neill and his troops were able to use their intimate knowledge of the landscape to great advantage. He rendered impotent their cavalry and cut away at their rearguard.

Bagnall is said to have been shot through the head by a fair-haired youth but his body disappeared. Many years later a skull was found in the Old Cathedral in Armagh; it had a hole through the centre of the forehead. The victory was commemorated by Barney O'Neill from Kilmore in a rarely heard verse of *The Boys from the County Armagh*:

I live in that part of the County
Where Bagnall the Great was o'er thrown,
Where the winding and murmuring Blackwater
Divides it from County Tyrone.

Barney O'Neill, like a number of other people, claimed to have written that iconic song but it seems the jury is firmly out on that one. In the 1920s, however, he did give the words – the rest of which differ only slightly from the 1950s recording of it – to a woman in Loughgall who was known for her singing.

Incidentally the other iconic song from the county is *The Bard of Armagh* and it records, albeit subtly, the difficult penal times. Many think it a much finer song than the previous one. One aspect of the Penal Laws, still operating in the early eighteenth century, was the banning of bishops, archbishops and friars on pain of transportation or death. What happened as a result was that bishops travelled in disguise, administering to their flock and sometimes ordaining priests. The Bard in the song was Bishop Patrick O'Donnelly, who suffered great hardships from the Penal Laws. He went under the name of Felim Brady and played the harp to pass himself off as a bard at fairs and weddings until his death in 1719. In the last verse of the song he uses a woman's name, 'Kathleen', as a metaphor for Ireland. For hundreds of years when sentiments of patriotism were an offence, a woman's name was used by poets to represent Ireland as the loved one (e.g. *Mo Roisín Dubh* – My Dark Rosaleen). The poet and playwright W.B. Yeats used it in his play *Cathleen Ní Houlihan*. So when the Bard says 'In the arms of my Kathleen, my dear wife oh lay me', he's referring simply to burial in Ireland. Although

the last line is 'Forget Felim Brady the Bard of Armagh', the song
ensures that he is immortalised.

> Oh list to the tune of a bold Irish harper
> And scorn not the strains of his old withered hand
> But remember his fingers could once move more swiftly
> to raise the merry strains of his own native land.
> At a wedding or fair I could wield my shillelagh
> And dance through a jig with my boots bound with straw
> While all the pretty maidens around me assembled
> Loved bold Felim Brady, the Bard of Armagh.
> And when sergeant death puts his cold arms around me
> and lays me to rest in sweet Erin go breá,
> By the side of my Kathleen, my dear wife, oh lay me
> And forget Felim Brady, the Bard of Armagh.

Patrick O'Donnelly hid out on the slopes of Slieve Gullion but
back to Loughgall to when the O'Neill lands were redistributed.
There was huge resentment which, of course, presented its own
problems to the people who were 'gifted' land. Colonisation was
causing the same issues in many parts of the world during that
period. Bitterness softened and sharpened through the centuries
according to the will and sense of justice of the people. There was
an appalling flare up in the eighteenth century with competition
over the linen industry when the Peep O'Day boys operated and
the Defenders was formed. Atrocity bred atrocity as always and the
Orange Order was formed in 1795. It seems that any good will or
wish for coexistence dissolved after that. It's estimated that 4,000
refugees from County Armagh fled to County Mayo in 1796.

Dan Winter's Cottage in Loughgall marks the place where
the earliest meeting for the formation of the Orange Order
took place (though that's disputed). The house dates back to the
mid-eighteenth century and the Winter family has taken great
care to retain many aspects of it. As well as being of interest to

the Orange Order, much of what it contains is of interest to the general public. Hilda Winter has preserved house and farm implements and even baby clothing; in fact she has created something of a country museum and she is very welcoming and more than willing to relate the history of the family and surroundings.

The trees of this area bear bitter fruit and many find that profitable but there is sweet fruit too. In the twentieth century a friendship grew between a Mr Mayes, a minister in Kilmore, and Fr Donnelly, a priest in Stonebridge. When Mr Mayes was retiring and a collection was being made, Fr Donnelly, who had been transferred to The Loop in County Derry, was the first person to contribute. He was also the first person that Mr Mayes mentioned in his retirement speech, which was reported in the paper. The sacristan, Tommy McClelland, sent the cutting on to Fr Donnelly, who wrote back a letter of thanks.

A Loughgall local told me about another occasion when Mr Mayes made an impression. In the primary school in Kilmore they had a Christmas tree event every year. The parents came to the school and a prize was given to the winner in each class. The prize was a bible and one year my informant's sister, a Catholic, won the prize. Mr Mayes had the sensitivity to enquire what book she used at church on Sunday and he went off to Bennetts in Armagh and bought one which he inscribed for her.

In a strange twist of events, he moved to Armagh City as an elderly man in poor health and that same little girl, by then a nurse, ended up caring for him in the last period of his life.

There's hope for us all yet.